KIRSTY LOGAN

Kirsty Logan is the author of the novels *The Gracekeepers* and *The Gloaming*, the short story collections *A Portable Shelter* and *The Rental Heart and Other Fairytales*, the flash fiction chapbook *The Psychology of Animals Swallowed Alive*, and the short memoir *The Old Asylum in the Woods at the Edge of the Town Where I Grew Up*. Her books have won the Lambda Literary Award, the Polari First Book Prize, the Saboteur Award, the Scott Prize and the Gavin Wallace Fellowship, and been selected for the Radio 2 Book Club and the Waterstones Book Club. Her short fiction and poetry have been translated into Japanese and Spanish, recorded for radio and podcasts, exhibited in galleries and distributed from a vintage Wurlitzer cigarette machine. She lives in Glasgow with her wife and their rescue dog.

ALSO BY KIRSTY LOGAN

KIRSTY LOGAN

Things We Say in the Dark

VINTAGE

3 5 7 9 10 8 6 4 2

Vintage
20 Vauxhall Bridge Road,
London SW1V 2SA

Vintage is part of the Penguin Random House group of companies
whose addresses can be found at global.penguinrandomhouse.com

Penguin
Random House
UK

Copyright © Kirsty Logan Limited 2019

Kirsty Logan has asserted her right to be identified as the
author of this Work in accordance with the Copyright,
Designs and Patents Act 1988

Ilustrations by Nora Dåsnes

First published in Vintage in 2020
First published in hardback by Harvill Secker in 2019

penguin.co.uk/vintage

A CIP catalogue record for this book is available
from the British Library

ISBN 9781529111286

Printed and bound in Great Britain by Clays Ltd, Elcograf S.p.A.

Penguin Random House is committed to a sustainable future
for our business, our readers and our planet. This book is
made from Forest Stewardship Council® certified paper.

To Kay Ckface, Susie-poo and Alice Nimoysdóttir
– for everything you said to me in September 2016

Contents

CONTENTS

PART 1:
THE HOUSE

'One need not be a chamber to be haunted.'
- Emily Dickinson

I wrote much of my last book during a writing retreat in the middle of a forest in Finland. For this book, I spent a month in Iceland on a retreat that was similar, except even more isolated, with even fewer people around. I know that for many people, going away means chasing the sun, but I've always been more of a north person.

It was a strange time. I spent entire days in silence without seeing another living thing. When I walked into the local shop, I couldn't understand why people were looking at me, then quickly away – then I realised that I was silently mouthing my thoughts, like I sometimes do when I'm writing. It was weird and I got sad and I lost myself a little and through it all I wrote, I wrote so much.

I don't know what I was trying to say, but whatever it was, I tried my best to say it.

Even as all the strangeness was happening – even as I lost myself, even as I forgot how to speak, even as I was more alone than I had ever been – I wasn't afraid.

I knew that I had a home to go back to. Four walls for protection, for confinement. For better, or for worse.

So here we go, into the dark.

Last One to Leave Please Turn Off the Lights

First Fear:

The first house I gave you was a tooth. The dentist pulled it to make space for the rest of my teeth, which apparently is often a problem for small-mouthed people when the wisdom teeth come in. He asked if I wanted the tooth, and I didn't particularly, but I also didn't want it to get thrown in the bin, so I wrapped it in a tissue and took it home. It was jagged at one end and it smelled sweet and a bit rotten. I got a nail from the toolbox and started to carve. I'll admit it wasn't worth putting in an art gallery, but by the end of the day my tooth was a tiny though recognisable house. I understand that when I presented it to you, half joking, as we were brushing our teeth before bed, it was unexpected. You seemed pleased at the gesture, if a little disgusted. It wasn't your fault that the tooth got knocked into the toilet and accidentally flushed.

The second house I braided from my hair. There was a reasonable amount in my hairbrush, but not enough. I pulled out more from all over my head so that I wouldn't leave any obvious bald patches. My hair is long and thick so I got two good handfuls without it looking much different, and its stiff curl meant it took to braiding well. The walls and roof were dense, and I even managed two windows. I shouldn't have surprised you by putting the hair next to your morning cup of coffee. As I was falling asleep the night before it had seemed quirky and charming, but I see now that it was a weird thing to do and made you not want to eat your scrambled eggs. It wasn't your fault that the coffee got spilled, making the house dampen and fold in on itself and collapse into a mat of tangles. When you left for work I threw the hair out of the kitchen window. I like to think of it, this little perfect house I made – for you from me – caught on a breeze, tugged quick to the sky, blown off a bridge to float down the river.

The third house was my fingernails. They made a beautiful roof, prettier than any tiles I've seen, each one painted a different colour. I only have ten nails so the roof was very small. It wasn't your fault that it somehow got put in the food scraps bin along with the onion skin and the carrot peels and the chicken bones.

That gave me an idea, and the next house was carved from the bone of my little finger. It was accidentally fed to the dog. My ear-house got buried in the window box; my eye-house was squashed under your winter boots; my tongue-house was snatched by a neighbourhood fox.

I made you house after house after house. But each time it was too small, too losable, too easily destroyed.

Finally, there I stand in front of you, everything removable or soft in me gone. I have made this final house for you: the rafters my ribs, the floor my flattened feet, the overhead light my unblinking eye. Come lie on the couch of the long bone of my thigh. Come rest your head on the cushion of my slow-beating heart. Come home.

Second Fear:

May visited her friend Blank in his new house. He made tea and laid out a plate of biscuits and told May how important a good house was, how you couldn't be a real human without one. Their other friend Ambrosia agreed, and told May that she should be working as hard as she could so that she could buy a house instead of just a flat. May dipped her biscuit in her tea and didn't reply.

The next week, Blank and Ambrosia visited May at her flat. She bought special biscuits and used her best crockery. Her friends perched on the edge of her threadbare couch and held their tea without sipping it. Blank observed, ever so politely, that May's flat was very small and needed many repairs: the damp patches on the ceiling, the dripping tap in the bathroom, the chipped paint in the hall. Ambrosia observed, even more politely, that she didn't have thick carpets or heavy wallpaper or curtains in the windows, only roller blinds, and they weren't enough to block out the flashing lights from the street, and there wasn't enough noise-reduction, and her ceilings were too low so when the upstairs neighbour walked across the floor in high heels it sounded like she was click-clacking on your forehead. All things considered, May's flat was too small, too spare, too full of cracks. The outside world encroached far too much. Blank and Ambrosia didn't stay long.

May did want to please her friends. She didn't have enough money to fix all the problems with her flat, or to buy anything new to go inside it, or to move out and into a house. But May was clever. She found a solution.

The dollhouse sat nicely on her shoulders – not too heavy, but reassuringly weighty. She piled her hair up and pinned it on top of her head so it filled the attic, holding the house steady. Her eyes lined up perfectly with the upstairs windows, the house only restricting her vision as much as a pair of spectacles. And if she wanted to speak, she could just open the front door.

The dollhouse was much easier to maintain than her flat. When it was windy and a few miniature tiles fell off - well, she just got them replaced with squares of painted card. The hammering of the tiny tacks gave her a headache, but she posted painkillers through the letter box and into her mouth, and the pain soon faded. When the gutters couldn't handle the damp autumn leaves - well, she just put on rubber gloves and scooped the rotting mush out herself. When she discovered a wasps' nest in her hair - well, yes, that was a bit of a problem. The exterminator said that the house must be evacuated before it could be fumigated, but it wasn't as simple as that for May. Finally the exterminator agreed to sort the wasps' nest with her still inside. She wasn't stupid, though; she wore a mask. It was fine. Everything was fine.

The dollhouse blocked sound beautifully, so May kept it on all the time, even when she was sleeping. She liked being inside the house while also being inside her flat; it was cosier that way, safer. There was no need to get curtains for her flat - why, with the doll-house shutters closed she couldn't see anything at all, no matter how many flashing lights went by outside. She didn't need to put the heating on - her hands and feet and body were cold, but her head was always toasty-warm. She got the flat's electricity shut off too - she didn't need it, as the dollhouse had the most delightful little battery-operated lights.

Perhaps May did get the house just to please her friends, but now that she had it she realised that they were right all along. Her house did make her happy. Unfortunately, Blank and Ambrosia were not impressed. Fortunately, May didn't care. She was tired of seeing their disapproving looks. She was tired of opening her mouth to explain herself.

She closed the window shutters and locked the front door. Just to be sure, she swallowed the key and nailed the shutters. See? It's warm in here. Dark and safe and cosy. Just don't look outside. It's fine. Everything is fine.

Third Fear:

Since the moment you were born, you haven't felt quite right, have you? The world looms. It's all too big, too much. Let's not even talk about anything outside the world; a single photo of outer space can make you unsteady for days.

Kristin understood; she felt the same as you. When she looked up, the sky was so far away it made her stagger. When she was in a car or a train or a plane, the world seemed to stretch out around her forever. When she thought of what she – and probably you – had learned at school, about the universe and its vastness, the infinity of it, the insignificant tininess of her within it, it made her sick and cold and dizzy.

Since being born, the only time Kristin came close to finding peace was when she had her own child, her own confinement. A baby instantly becomes its mother's whole world, tiny and beautifully manageable. The stony weight of the growing foetus in Kristin helped, but even more than that was the sameness of her days after the birth, the feeling of the walls closing in around her. It was hard to go anywhere with a newborn, or even with a toddler, or even with a ten-year-old. They're so heavy, and all they need is one unobserved second to dash away. Reins can snap and Calpol isn't that strong, really, no matter how many doses the child swallows. Better to just stay inside, in the tiny flat, in the tiny cupboard turned into a nursery.

Kristin's next confinement was prison. There's no need to go into the details – she wasn't there for so long, but it was long enough. Such a pleasantly graspable world with its timetables and routines. The first time she was locked in her cell, she was surprised by her sense of peace. Her sheets were red like her insides and the walls were soft and stained pink with damp. At night she was sure she could hear them breathe. The heating throbbed like a heart. She felt so peaceful that she wanted to die.

But when she'd done her time, they opened the door and pushed her out. She stepped past the prison gate and fell to the ground. The sky was so far away and the world stretched forever and there was nothing steady to hold on to. She wanted to crouch in the footwell of the car and have someone put a blanket over her. A wooden board. A locked door.

Kristin tried to live a regular life for a time, but soon found she couldn't bear it. She needed to be able to touch the sides of her world. Everything was so vast and she felt that her body would jolt apart and float off into space. She was always cold. She took all the money she had and paid to have a tiny place made. Some people might call it a cupboard, an anchorage, or a grave; for Kristin, it was the perfect house, made just for her, the walls just wider than her shoulders and the ceiling just higher than her head. She said goodbye to the world she had known: good riddance to cold drinks on hot days, to slotting the final piece into a jigsaw, to the rush and sudden chill of an orgasm with a stranger. She went home and asked you to help her. After all, she'd helped to keep you confined and safe, hadn't she? The least you could do was return the favour.

So here we are. You feel the rough bricks in your hand. The trowel smoothing on the cement. It's no surprise that you'd be the one who'd end up bricking Kristin in. You always did have to snap the reins and spit out the Calpol. Why are you like this? You're leaning hard on the wall as you work and your hands are shaking. The flat felt small and safe and solid when you first arrived but now it's getting bigger, flimsier. The ceiling seems further away than before. Is that sky you can see through the rafters? Don't breathe so hard, you're making the walls shake.

Only a few bricks to go. From inside her new tiny house, Kristin hums a happy song.

You hear her shift around, getting comfortable. But if she can move, then there is extra space, isn't there? Too much space. Clearly this tiny house is not meant for her. You are a little taller than Kristin, a little wider. Perhaps the extra of you is for the extra space in there.

You pull Kristin out of the house and climb inside. You brick up the door behind you. She can scream and beg all she wants, but she is still outside and you are still inside.

It's dark in here, and good. You don't feel sick. The ceiling is the height of you. The walls are the width of you. You see the boundaries now, and you can stop.

Fourth Fear:

There was no one else to clear out the house other than Lydia. Her sisters Barbara and Delia weren't even in the country - one in Brooklyn on an internship, one in London doing something stressful in media. Why make them come all the way home just to clear out an old man's house? Not that he was just any old man.

But, to be honest, Lydia didn't want her grampa's stuff any more than Barbara or Delia did.

She wandered the house, feeling unhaunted. Yes, she'd learned to play on this piano. Yes, she'd watched Saturday-morning TV on this couch. Yes, she'd eaten porridge off these spoons and speared peas with these forks. Should she take them? But she already had spoons and forks and a couch, and she liked them better than these ones. With her grampa gone, the things were just things.

She stripped the beds and tugged the clothes off their hangers. She pulled open the drawers and cupboards. She opened all the windows to let the summer air get in and around and behind all the things. She liked the smell of her grampa, but the person who bought the house probably would not.

Before Lydia could deal with the things, she had to deal with the ashes. She decided to scatter them by the greenhouse, where she used to help her grampa with the tomatoes. The stalks were withered now, the growbags dried up, but she could still smell the warm greenness on the air.

The urn was made of thick plastic, heavier than she expected. She stood by the greenhouse with the urn in her hands and she thought about her grampa. She missed him, of course she did. He was good, but he was gone, and not wanting to stand there for another ten minutes didn't mean she loved him any less.

She was surprised, on opening the urn's lid, to find that the ashes were gold. Clearly he was very good indeed. But, still, he was gone. She tipped the urn to let the ashes fall – but just at that moment, a breeze caught the whole scattering lot and blew it through the open windows and into the house.

Lydia stood for a long time, the upturned urn in her hands, the breeze playing through her hair. Then she held her breath and went inside.

She needn't have worried: she was not about to inhale her grampa. All the things in the house - the carpets, the lightshades, the sideboard, the dining table, the floral three-piece suite, the bonbon dish in the shape of an elephant, the china shepherdess, the magazine rack, the kettle, the shower head, the ugly faïence fruit bowl that didn't have any fruit in it, the bar of soap by the sink, the mattress, the fridge - every single thing was covered in gold.

Not coated in gold. Not gold-plated. But scattered with enough tiny dots of gold that, in the bright summer sun, everything glittered.

Lydia rubbed at the surface of the fridge with her fingertip. The gold didn't come off. She scratched it with her nail. It still didn't come off. Over the next few hours, Lydia scraped and scrubbed and gouged at every gold thing in the house, which was everything. The gold stayed.

She called her sisters. Barbara wanted her to call the house clearance company, just like they'd planned before. Delia thought that was ridiculous - it was covered in gold, for heaven's sakes! It was valuable now. And not just valuable in a nostalgic sort of way, because they'd learned to play on that piano and stuff. She wanted Lydia to sell the golden things. Lydia hung up the phone.

She closed all the golden windows and made up all the golden beds and put the golden clothes back on their golden hangers. Then she stood in the middle of the golden house looking at the ugly faïence fruit bowl. She couldn't throw it away, because it was valuable. She couldn't sell it, because it was her grampa. She couldn't keep it, because she already had a fruit bowl she liked better and her grampa was gone and keeping his fruit bowl wouldn't bring him back.

She pictured herself carrying all the golden things out of her grampa's house and trying to fit them into her own small flat; how every wall and surface would be covered past using, every blink blinding gold. She pictured herself living here, making a life among the remnants of her grampa. Sleeping on the mattress of him, washing in the bath of him, using the spoons of him to eat her cereal.

Lydia stood there in the golden hallway, looking at the golden fruit bowl. The longer she stood there, the heavier it felt. Was it her imagination, or were the walls beginning to sag? Could the floor joists take the weight of all this gold?

The sun began to set. The light through the windows made the whole house sparkle.

Not long before I started this book, my wife and I got married in a library. She wore vintage brogues and a pinstriped suit; I wore a feathered cape and a grey silk dress. We wanted our wedding to be special and different, just like everyone wants their wedding to be special and different. But like everyone, we slipped into cliché: it was magical and all our living parents cried and I had probably the happiest day of my life.

We went on a northern honeymoon, where we kissed on black-sand beaches under the slow green throb of the northern lights and felt a constant bone-deep cold, colder than we'd ever been in our lives.

We did the expected thing, and bought a home. We spent a lot of time looking at paint charts and debating different kitchen work-tops. I've never felt so steady, so domesticated.

That's why I decided I was ready to write about my fears. I have a place to retreat to where I can always put on the lights no matter how dark it is outside.

Things My Wife and I Found Hidden in Our House

1. A RING

And isn't that sweet? Isn't it just too perfectly sweet, like it's a message of hope left for me and Alice, a blessing for our life together?

I caught the ring with the edge of the broom as I was sweeping out the kitchen. It scraped along the tiles and made a hell of a racket. At first I thought it was just rubbish, all clarty with grot and bugs, but when I rinsed it under the tap it came up lovely. A little circlet of glass, green as a summer sea, bright on its surface but with shadows at its centre. I thought maybe Alice's granny had left it for us on purpose. Maybe she wasn't so bad after all.

This was her house, before, and it's not that she didn't know that we were together, but it was complicated. She called me Alice's friend, and I could hear the way she put inverted commas around it, even after Al and I had lived together for years and we'd both visited her a thousand times in this musty old house that always smelled like the sea even though it was miles from water.

I slid the ring onto my wedding finger then raced through the house, calling for Alice, and found her in the spare bedroom with her arms full of floral duvets.

'These are going straight to the tip,' she said. 'Can you smell that? They're damp. Damn, I hope it's not in the walls.'

'Look, Al!' I held out my hand, queen-like. 'Isn't this pretty? Your gran must have left it.'

She peered at it. 'Is it plastic? It looks like it came out of a vending machine. Throw it away, there's enough junk in this house already.'

'It's sea-glass. I found it in the kitchen. Do you think it's a good-luck charm from your gran? To wish us well?'

Alice threw the musty duvets into the hall. 'Trust me, Rain. My gran didn't wish anybody well.'

2. PAPER

The folded page fell when we bashed the frame of the front door trying to carry the old bath out. I know, I know, we should have hired someone, but to be honest what little money we had was tied up in the house. Turns out, just because you inherit something, doesn't mean you get it for free. Alice tucked the paper in her pocket and then, when I was driving to the tip, the bath awkwardly wedged between the boot and the back seat, she pulled the paper out and unfolded it. It was as yellow as old bones and smelled musty-sweet.

'What does it say?'

Alice didn't reply.

I stopped the car at a red light.

'Hello! Are you listening?'

'It says ...' she said. 'No, it's nothing.' And she balled up the paper and put it in the glove compartment.

'Al, stop being weird! What does it say?'

'KELPIES TO HELL,' she said.

I wasn't sure whether to laugh. 'What's a kelpie?' Alice didn't reply, so added: 'Call me a Sassenach if you like, just tell me.'

'A kelpie is a mythical creature,' Alice said, frowning. 'Lives in lochs. It's a horse and also a beautiful woman. If it doesn't like you, it drags you into the water and drowns you.'

'O ... kay,' I said. 'But why would your gran want to tell us that?'

'Jesus, Rain, would you drop it with the secret messages? My gran was losing it towards the end. She didn't know I was going to get the house. She didn't know I was going to live here with you. None of this means anything, okay?'

So I drove the rest of the way to the tip in silence, and together we lifted the bath where Alice's granny had had a stroke and drowned, and we threw it away.

3. A HORSE

Alice found this one. It was the size of a thumb, wedged into the skirting board under the bed. She brought it to the kitchen as I was making tea and said: 'Rain, I can't find my glasses. Can you read this?'

I rubbed the tiny horse's haunches, feeling the symbols etched into the copper.

'It's not words,' I said. 'It's runes or something. Maybe it's an old Highlands superstition, and your gran left it to protect us from being trampled by - well, not a horse, but - life? Sadness? Money worries?'

Alice raised her eyebrows. 'Well, my mum always did say my gran was a witch. She stole my grandad from another woman - did

I ever tell you that?' Alice took the horse from my hand. 'He was married to someone else when they met. A woman always dressed in green, who wore strange jewellery, rings made of glass she found washed up on the beach. She had green eyes and long black hair - black as a winter night, black like it was always wet.'

My eyes were wide. 'What happened?'

'My gran went round to talk to her, to say, basically, I want your man and there's nothing you can do about it, and she must have been pretty convincing because the next day the woman was gone. She left the village - went for a job down south or something. But you know the strange thing? No one ever saw that woman again.'

'Oh my God!' I said. 'Did your gran - do you think she - could she have done something?'

Alice laughed. 'Come on, Rain! What, you think my wee old granny was a murderer?'

'Why not? Every murderer has a family.'

'It's just a silly story,' Alice said. 'Gran obviously didn't kill anyone. She was the other woman, so she had to make up stories about my grandad's ex. Make her into a spooky witch, a baddie, not a poor lass who'd had her man stolen. If the first wife was the villain, then Gran was the hero, and she could feel better. Simple as that. And she—' At this Alice jerked her hand and dropped the horse. It thudded to the floor and skittered away.

All I could do was stare at the blistered outline of the copper horse burned into Alice's palm.

4. PEARLS

It was boring, dirty work, doing up the house. Alice's gran hadn't touched anything in years - aside from hiding weird things in grubby corners, apparently. There was so much to do that Alice and I always ended up working late into the night, holding off the dark as best we could. Alice's blistered hand was healing, but slowly, and I'd got a nasty scrape up my calf from a cluster of nails left inexplicably spiked through a cupboard door.

When I found the long string of pearls on top of the wardrobe, I stripped off all my clothes and stepped into the shower – then stepped back out and wrapped the pearls around my neck. They were as long as a bridle; I looped them three times and they still covered my breasts. I stood under the hot water until I couldn't see for steam, then I walked, still dripping, into the kitchen where Alice was fixing the radiator.

'What do you think I should do with—' she said, and then she saw me and dropped the spanner. We made love on a clean dust sheet on the kitchen counter, and afterwards, Alice whispered in my ear: 'That's how you catch a kelpie, you know. With a string of pearls around its neck. My grandad told me – he caught a kelpie once. You catch it, and then it has to love you forever.' She rolled on top of me and kissed me hard, so hard the pearls pressed red circles into my sweat-damp skin, so hard my teeth nicked bloody on the inside of my mouth.

5. HAIR

We'd plumbed in the new bath, and I christened it that night with candles and bath oil. I never felt clean in this house; we'd scrubbed every inch but still kept catching this smell, rancid and salt-heavy like old seaweed. Although I hadn't said anything to Alice, I was worried that there was damp in the walls, the house rotten to the core.

I filled the bath full of the hottest water I could stand and slid right down, my nose the only dry part. I felt my muscles relax into liquid and heard my heart boom, boom, boom, steady as footsteps, steady as hoofbeats– And then there was nothing holding me up, and I was underwater, water in my nose, water in my mouth, and I couldn't breathe, and I couldn't find the sides to pull myself out and I felt water in my throat, water in my lungs, and I sank down into the darkness.

Then Alice was pulling me out and I was crouching on the bathroom floor, coughing up water, breath rasping, and there was something wrong with my hand, something tight and tickling, and I reached for Alice, and my fist was wrapped all around with layers of hair. Long black hair, black as a winter night, and as long as a horse's mane.

6. A GLASS JAR

At first, I couldn't tell what was inside. When I pulled it out of the dim hidden place inside the bathroom wall, I thought it was jam. Beneath its jacket of dust, it looked plum-dark and sticky. My tongue tingled; I thought about toast and tea and the sweet smear of berries, sitting in the sun with Alice, the sound of her laugh. But that was silly: it was too late for sun, and Alice hadn't laughed for a long time.

I shook the jar and felt the thing inside smack off the glass, the wet press of meat. I gave the jar to Alice. She went to unscrew the lid, then thought better.

She looked at it for a long time. 'It's a liver,' she said.

'A what?' I asked, because I'd heard but I wished I hadn't. In Alice's shaking grip, the purplish thing in the jar quivered.

'It's what the kelpie leaves,' Alice said, and her voice didn't sound right. 'It drags you to the bottom of the loch and eats you, every single bit of you except your liver. If you find a liver on the shore, that's how you know the kelpie has eaten someone.'

7. A KNIFE

I wasn't surprised when Alice and I found the long thin silver knife wrapped in blackened grot beneath the floorboards. It wasn't easy: to find it we'd had to pull up just about every rotting, stinking board in the house, our hands slick with blood and filth. Alice had told me that a silver knife through the heart is the only way to kill a kelpie, so if Alice's gran really had killed it, the knife was likely to be there somewhere. Her mistake, her haunting, was in keeping the thing. As proof? A memento? We'd never know. Then again, we knew that her bathtub drowning was due to a stroke. So I guess you can never really know anything.

Alice and I gathered up the ring and the paper and the horse and the pearls and the hair and the glass jar and the knife, and we put them all in a box. We drove for hours until we got to the coast, to the town where Alice's gran and her grandad and the first wife had all lived, and we climbed to the highest cliff and we threw all the things into the sea.

Together we drove back to the house, holding hands between the front seats. A steady calm grew in our hearts; we knew that it was over, that we had cleansed the house and ourselves, that we had proven women's love was stronger than women's hate.

8. MORE

Approaching the front door, key outstretched, hands still held, hearts grown sweet, Alice and I stopped. Our hands unlinked. The doorknob was wrapped all around with layers of long black hair.

A house is family. A house is history. A house is a body. One subject that comes up again and again in horror, both new and classic, is houses. Haunted houses, home invasions, axe murderers lurking in the attics and chasing us into the basements. Our homes are a site of endless terror.

We are afraid that someone will come into our house when we don't want them to. We are afraid that the thing we fear is already inside. We are afraid that we can't make it leave. We are afraid that the lock on the door will not hold.

My House is Out Where the Lights End

E veryone said that sunflowers couldn't grow this far north and they were right, they couldn't and wouldn't, until finally, one day, they did. Pop always said it was because of his Secret Method. He said it in capital letters to make it sound scientific and complicated, but Jay and Yara watched him in secret from Jay's bedroom window and knew exactly what his method was: he sang to the sunflowers. Big Pop, terror of the town, half the teeth smacked out of his head, body more scars than skin, faster with his fists than a kung-fu movie star. Big Pop sang to the flowers.

Jay thinks now that she should have found that sweet. Her father, a surprise like a wrapped present, hard as nails but soft as trifle – it was sweet, right? But at the time she found it frightening that Pop was so unpredictable. That he could be two opposite things at once. That there was no way to know whether it would be fists or song.

She drives up to the old farmhouse with her sunglasses on and the radio off. In her memory it looms so huge, so loud and technicolour, that she's sure it will overwhelm everything else. But the bright painted boards are faded and rain-dragged, and the tin roof is rusted through in places, and the driveway is overgrown with weeds. She pulls the car to a jolting stop and sits there, watching the empty house as if waiting for someone to come out and get her. No one does.

She climbs out of the car and walks round to the back of the house, where in her memory miles of sunflowers gleam brighter than the sun. She finds a field of withered grey stalks, bent under the weight of their dead heads. The ground is heaving with black seeds, piled thick, gleaming like insect shells. She kicks at them and listens to them sift, an uncomfortably sensual sound. For many seasons the field must have grown wild, alone all summer, then sunk back on itself through autumn, only to repeat the whole thing again next year. A ghost harvest.

She shoulders aside a dead sunflower to go further into the field and jerks back with a cry when a smatter of small black somethings land on her shoulder. She stands on open ground, shuddering, brushing off her bare shoulder long after she's seen that it was just sunflower seeds, dead black carapaces now scattered in the dirt around her feet. She knows they just fell from the head when she knocked it, but she can't stop thinking of the word *spat*, that the sunflower spat the seeds at her on purpose.

Jay goes to the back door of the house, faltering on the steps when she feels the lack of a key in her hand. Then she shakes her head, laughing at herself: city girl. All through her childhood this door was never locked, and she and Yara clattered in and out all summer, the door banging in its frame, the checked curtain whipping in the breeze. Now that she looks at the door, it doesn't even have a keyhole; it's just a brass housing and a handle, like on an internal door. Everything is rotted to hell; the wood is soft and yielding under her hand, and the door creaks open easily. The floor is more dirt than lino. The sink, the oven, the cabinets: everything ripped out and taken away.

On late summer days Jay and Yara used to go exploring, eating blackberries straight from the bush, even though Mam said they were covered in fox piss. They'd stay out collecting berries so late that the sun went down and the light dropped blue and the owls swooped over their heads, making them run shrieking with laughter through the bramble-choked lanes. When they got home their arms were all scratches and their bellies ached from eating too many berries. Mam said they were sick because of the fox piss, and didn't that just show them that it wasn't safe for girls out there, and that the world was a sickening place, and they were to be home before dusk from now on. Jay and Yara laughed – quietly, under the covers where Mam couldn't hear – oooh, the dangers of the owl were terrible, and oooh, the brambles were deadlier than the devil, and oooh, fox piss was coming in the night to get the softest girls.

Years after she grew up and left the farm, Jay was in a bar, cigarette in hand and onto her fifth beer, and she mentioned to some pretty bit of rough the name of her home town. Where all those folk went missing, said the pretty bit. Jay laughed and waved her beer bottle like she was stirring cake mix and said nah, it's a boring old town, nothing ever happened there but scarecrows and fox piss. The pretty bit laughed in that way you do when you're not sure if something is a joke. But Jay stubbed out her cigarette and turned sickly away because yes, people had gone missing, she remembered that now, at the time it had been in the papers and on people's lips but she hadn't cared.

She and Yara had been so busy in those days, preoccupied with hating their mother and pretending they were from a big city and trying to get their hair to do things it wouldn't and wanting their periods to come and then wanting their periods to go away. She'd always had a thought that her tiny shitty town might some day be known for her; that she'd do something amazing and when anyone heard the name of the town they'd say yeah, isn't that where Jay Kelly grew up? And instead it's known for nothing at all. Just some people whose names she can't even remember, if she ever knew them at all.

Jay goes into the living room. It's thick with shadows and she rips a sheet of newspaper off the window and lets in beams of dusty light. She's not the first one in here; there's a bucket with the remains of a fire in the middle of the room, and empty beer cans are snowpiled in the corners.

Some dark nights, Pop used to tell them ghost stories. Inside there was a fire and hot chocolate and pyjamas, and outside there was rain. He told them all the classic stories: the hook, the rat, the babysitter, the licked hand, the phantom hitchhiker. Mam would be annoyed that he was winding up the girls before bed, because she'd be the one who'd have to deal with the nightmares, but in the end she would settle down to listen too. In the gaps between Pop's words and the rain, Jay was sure she could hear the sunflowers growing, the slow creak of their stalks like someone calling out to her.

Jay opens the door to the cellar, but she doesn't go down the steps because she's not a fucking moron. It's gloomy and there's no electricity and the steps are probably rotted through. Even from up here she can smell the stink of it: wet earth, old blood, secret rot.

For a while Pop had turned the cellar into a mushroom farm. That sounds like it was a well-considered plan but it wasn't; one day he found a crop of mushrooms sprouting in the corner of the cellar's dirt floor, and he figured if they were already growing then he could make them grow more. Didn't everyone complain all the time that this country was rotten with damp? Might as well make the most of it.

He spent a whole season encouraging the mushrooms, fertilising the earth under the house with bonemeal and glass jars of frothing blood, which was a strange thing to be able to buy, Jay thought now, but she supposes he must have bought it all from somewhere. He hadn't checked before he grew the mushrooms which were the edible kind and which were the poisonous kind; he just increased what was already growing there. Every dinner time Jay would fear mushroom soup, mushroom pie, mushrooms chopped and blended in secret into everything she ate.

But she got tired of being afraid and chose instead to laugh. She and Yara decided that Pop was growing magic mushrooms, and they'd egg each other on to go and steal some so they could take them together. They wanted to lean back on the soft pillows of Jay's bed and hallucinate freely, see new worlds blossom and flower around them as outside the sunflowers nodded and the scarecrows crept closer and their father sang, sang, all through the night. They wanted to take horror and flip it into magic, fantasy: just stories they could tell from another life.

So in the autumn gloaming Jay and Yara had crept down the creaking cellar steps, ready for dares, ready to open new worlds – and found nothing but bare earth, the mushroom harvest gone. Pop had sold them, or given them away, or eaten them all himself, leaving nothing they could make a story from.

Jay's first job out of school was at a mushroom farm, a proper industrial one with flickering fluorescent lights and the choking smell of dried pigs' blood and the dirt sucking at her boots as she tried to pick enough mushrooms to fill her container to the top so that she would have enough money for her rent. After her shift, she shucked off the heavy white boots and the thick white suit in the staffroom, replaced them with her thin ballet pumps and her black jeans and vest. She felt so light and so dark, insubstantial, like she could slip into the shadows and no one would notice.

She remembers those times as being always night, always sitting gritty-eyed on the night bus with city lights swooping yolky past the window, always in that place between waking and sleeping. She didn't sleep much then. Partly because she took on as many shifts as she could at the mushroom farm, but also because even when she got back to her tiny studio flat and fell into bed, she had such awful dreams. The dreams seemed to come before she'd fallen asleep, and they were always of the sunflowers, their heavy heads like hoods on drooping necks, their leaves twitching like hands.

Jay goes up the stairs carefully, catching her breath at every creak, but the old treads hold. The landing window is spider-webbed with cracks and she can't see the dead field she knows is out there. She remembers now that it wasn't the sunflowers that bothered her, but the scarecrows. Every time she looked she was sure that there were more than before. Now the sunflowers are withered and so are the scarecrows, all their clothes and flesh gone to leave the wooden crucifixes bare.

One night Yara was going out with her friends to see a film so she ran a bath, and just before the hot water ran out there was a splutter-splat and into the tub plopped a mess of tiny white bones, scraps of black velvet, and two rows of doll-like razor teeth. Yara came screeching out of the bathroom and Mam smacked her hard on the bare thigh, and told her to stop being such a princess and that there was no more hot water in the tank so she'd just have to wash in the water as it was. Jay can't remember now whether Mam scooped out the rotted bits of bat or not. She does remember that she made fun of Yara for weeks about her bat-bath. Though now she sees what she hadn't at the time: that bat was down to the bones, so couldn't have died in the water tank that day. They'd all been having bat-baths for weeks.

Jay goes into the bathroom. Or rather her head and upper body go in; she keeps her feet on the threshold because the floor of the bathroom is rotted, the boards smashed right through in places, the kitchen downstairs visible through the splinter-edged holes. Everything here has been ripped out too: the sink, the tub, even the toilet. The walls are gouged with holes and she figures maybe that was to get at the pipes, for copper or something.

She laughs then, out loud, standing there on the threshold, remembering the scrap-metal dealer in town whose sign was always getting the 's' stolen off it, and how much she and Yara used to laugh at that, though they had to spell out the word c-r-a-p as they didn't dare say it even when they didn't think Mam was listening.

One winter it got so cold and the wind blew through the gaps in the walls and everyone complained about it, even Mam. Pop didn't put in central heating or anything poncey like that – instead he built a thin inner wall of wooden matchboard, about a foot from the outside walls. It was warmer, afterwards, though the rooms were much smaller and they had to push all the furniture closer to the middle. There was no space to walk around it so you had to climb over everything all the time like you were playing The Floor is Lava.

But Jay didn't mind that: what she did mind was sitting with her back to the walls, because she knew how big the space between the walls was, and she knew that it was big enough for a person to stand in there. She taped squares of newspaper over all the knotholes in her bedroom walls so that nobody could put their eye to one and watch her sleep.

Jay goes into her bedroom. No bed, no posters pinned up, no line of trainers along the wall. Empty. She walks around the edge of the room, counting her steps, checking to see if the room is bigger than she remembers. When she was a child this house enclosed her whole world, everything she knew, everything she'd ever loved or hated; but also she felt trapped in it, held tight, her limbs stretching too wide for the walls. She reaches the empty space where the window used to be and looks out to the field of rotted sunflowers and straight away she's thrown back into the past.

The scratch of the straw against her skin as she hoisted the bodies up, the straw hands stroking the nape of her neck, the moans that she knew must be the wind but sounded closer and more alive, the booted legs bumping against her calves and trying to wrap around her ankles, the warmth of them. Pop telling her higher, lift higher, and she strained her arms as much as she could because they were heavy, much heavier than she thought they could be, and finally Pop got them tied to the crossbar and Jay could go inside.

At bedtime Jay would wait for Pop to come and tuck her in, which she desired and feared in equal parts, but she shouldn't have bothered because since he planted the sunflowers he was rarely ever in the house at all. When the moon came up and licked the world silver, Jay opened her window and anchored her feet against the bedstead and rested her belly on the splintery sill and closed her eyes and leaned right out so that she could hear Pop singing to the flowers and imagine that he was singing to her.

One night, driving home with Pop, the rain lashing and his breath steaming the windows and the smell of hops and fart filling the car – Jay didn't know whether to make a joke about that or just keep quiet – and the country lanes were winding hairpins and the hills left her tummy behind like a roller coaster. The trees seemed closer to the road than usual, like they were raising their arms to scoop her in and whisper secrets. Branches blatted along the roof of the car and wet leaves stroked Jay's window, and she wanted to roll it down, and she turned her eyes front to ask Pop if she could and a big black shape loomed up fast and *smack* against the car's front bumper and *thuck* over the bonnet and Jay screwed up her eyes so she wouldn't accidentally see anything in the wing mirror. The next second she snapped her eyes open and turned round in her seat but the road had doglegged and she couldn't see behind them.

A deer, Pop said, hands tight on the wheel.

But, Jay said.

A fucking deer, Jay, he said, it shouldn't have been on the road.

And perhaps that should have changed everything; perhaps she should have felt differently about her father then. Scared of him, or suddenly sure that he was a monster; or reassured, even, more trusting that she was a kid and he was a grown-up and he knew what was and was not a deer. But it didn't change anything. Why would it? They lived in the country, and it's all nature there. In nature, things die.

Jay goes back downstairs and through the kitchen and out of the house. She ducks her head and covers the back of her neck with her linked hands to protect it from skittering seeds and she goes into the sunflower field.

There are four crucifixes in the field but she only checks one. She digs a little way into the dry earth, feeling it stick under her nails and settle on her tongue. Her nail catches on something hard and she pulls it out.

A tooth.

It's big, a molar maybe. No filling.

It could be hers, or Yara's; sacrificed to the Tooth Fairy and buried out here for some reason. She digs further and finds another hard object; she scoops at it and her palms come up full of teeth, more than ever came out of her and Yara's mouths combined.

She puts her hand back and her fingers close around a hank of hair and she tugs it from the earth, thinking it still could be hers, it could be Mam's, remnants from a hairbrush or – the hair comes free and there's scalp attached, a rough square the size of a tea bag.

Everything is spinning and she hears the dead seeds clacking and the sunflowers creaking and the empty crucifixes leaning down towards her and she digs, she digs, and all the way down it's teeth and hair and bones and teeth and hair and bones and teeth and hair and

My wife has always been my first reader. When we met I was halfway through writing the first draft of a novel, and before going to sleep I'd read her a chapter as a bedtime story. She has a difficult job and by the end of the day is very tired, so if she didn't fall asleep while I was reading then I knew it was a good chapter.

When I started writing this book, I wanted to read the stories to her. I was proud of them and wanted her to love them, even though I know she doesn't like horror. She tried to listen. But she stopped me before the end of the first story.

Sleep, You Black-Eyed Pig, Fall into a Deep Pit of Ghosts

Night whispers. Ellen woke instantly, eyes wide, no fog. Her feet took her to the window. Her hands slid the sash up. From the smudged mass of trees came a suggestion of voices, clear and pointed as glass, all hiss and high vowels. Clouds of glossy insects flickered, reflecting the moonlight, becoming night again. Ellen leaned out of the window to try to see better, her feet straining on the floorboards, the sill pressing into the tops of her thighs. Somewhere in the shadows, shrill angles of silver. She held her breath and strained her eyes against the dark.

'Jenette?'

Spindled figures, limbs long and thin, on all fours. The light of them pulsed. The longer she looked, the closer they came. The outside wall was rough on her hand as she pushed her upper body further out of the window. Her bedroom was on the first floor, but the ground didn't look far. She could easily jump down. She'd probably fly. They'd probably all catch her.

She blinked hard until she was sure: every one of them was staring up at her window. They reached for her. Their silver fingers beckoned.

She pulled herself up to kneel on the windowsill. She could see them clearly. They were bright as mercury, except for their black eyes. Their faces were terrible and beautiful. Inside their narrow chests, their hearts throbbed so hard the skin pulsed. Their voices filled her head.

Ellen took a breath and tensed her thighs, ready to tip forwards out of the window and float down to them. Her knees grazed hot against the window frame, the air so cold it took her breath.

From downstairs, the creak of the front door, the click of Jenette's heels. Giggly drunken whispers, the thud of a body falling against a wall.

'Sorry, Ellen!' Jenette couldn't seem to decide whether to whisper or shout, and chose something both and neither.

Ellen froze, wide-eyed. Her bedroom door had warped in its frame, and it let in a glow around the edges. A line of warm light stretched across the floor, reaching out to her, just touching the tip of her bare toe.

Her toe.

Her foot.

What the hell was she doing?

She looked down at herself, barefoot and freezing and kneeling on the windowsill. She looked further down: the ground, twenty feet below, cold and solid and ready to snap her spine. She stumbled back off the sill, landing with a thump on her bedroom floor.

Without looking, she shut and latched the window, her hands shaking. She wished it had a lock, so she could hide the key from herself. She edged back to the glass and looked outside.

The black trees, the bright stars. She was awake. There was nothing.

Downstairs, the air in the kitchen felt warm, expectant, unfamiliar. Half the room was too bright, making Ellen squint, and half was in shadow.

'Hey, sick girl! Did we wake you from a dirty dream?' Ash was drunk; she could tell by his shifting eyes, his unsteady hand pouring the wine, the way he was shuffling his feet off the beat of the music.

'Mmm,' Ellen replied. 'Sort of.'

Jenette leaned up off the couch, sloppy-sexy, her lips shiny, and pulled Ellen over onto her lap. 'Poor wee beastie. Snuggle in, eh?'

'Get off, daft bugger.' Ellen laughed and pushed away from Jenette, but not too far. She settled on the couch, making sure her leg was pressed against Jenette's, and Jenette tipped Ellen's head onto her shoulder and stroked her hair.

'Soft,' she said. 'How do you get it so soft?'

'Get this down you. Warms the blood.' Ash swaggered over to the table and slapped down two overfull wine glasses. Ellen lifted one and sipped. Her head still throbbed with her fever, her skin too hot and too cold. With a laugh, Jenette leaned forward and licked the circular base of Ellen's glass, where a drop of wine threatened to fall.

Ellen settled her wine glass on her sternum, relaxing in to Jenette. She thought about tilting her head up and kissing her, but she didn't, not yet.

It felt like the right time, this trip. The thing between her and Jenette had been building for so long, and now they were here, playing house. Ten days off work, budget flights, this pretty little Finnish cabin surrounded by woods. Together, alone – and okay,

41

Ash was there too, technically, though he hardly counted. Ellen could feel him watching her with Jenette. She felt like someone would have to be blind not to see this thing between them, not to sense the build of it, the inevitable climax.

But she wouldn't kiss Jenette in front of Ash. She'd wait for the right time – under the northern lights, or in a forest clearing in the middle of a fairy ring. Somewhere epic and foreign and mythical.

'So what were they like?' Ellen asked. 'The neighbours?'

'Isn't it weird?' Ash said, flopping to the couch next to them, draping his leg over Jenette's, ignoring the roll of her eyes and the giggle into Ellen's hair. 'Isn't it the weirdest fucking thing? You build a holiday cabin right out in the middle of nowhere, and someone comes along and builds theirs next door. There's literally fucking miles of nothing, and that's what they do. Fucking people.'

'Come on, Ash! They were nice. Really, Ellen, they were nice.'

'Tell Ellen about the stories.'

'What stories?' Ellen was woozy from the fever and the wine. She could just fall asleep right there on the couch, with the heat of Jenette's skin and the rhythm of her breath.

'Weeeeird stories!'

'Ash, don't be a dick. They weren't weird. They were interesting.'

'Hmm?' Ellen said, which was all she could manage.

'It's like an old folk story,' Jenette said. 'They said that there are things hidden out here, and you don't see them until you're ready.'

'What do they look like?'

'No one knows,' Ash interrupted. 'Because once you see them, they get you, and no one ever sees you again. Woooooo!' He made ghost noises, waving his arms, spilling wine down himself. 'Spoooooooky!'

'Fuck off, Ash,' Jenette said, and lifted Ellen's hair to whisper in her almost-sleeping ear. 'They can be beautiful, the hidden things.

People see them because they want to. There are so many wonderful things, if we would only let ourselves see.'

Alone in her bed, Ellen wasn't alone for long. The first she knew was a soothing hand placed on her forehead. Thinking it was Jenette, she smiled through her fever. But it was not: the palm too cold, the fingers too long. Ellen's eyes were hot and weighted.

Before she could open them to look, the hand had moved, stroking the damp hair back from her face. Shhhh, tinkled a voice, shrill as silver. The hand kept stroking, and then it was joined by others.

Five, six, seven hands, smoothing back her hair. Then over her collarbones, cooling her hot skin. Pushing the covers down to her waist and further, further. The sweat on her skin turned to pearls and diamonds. Silver swirled behind her eyes. She was in the clouds, she was on a bed of leaves. Everything was cool and soft – and still the hands.

Ellen could hear herself breathing faster. The room was quiet: only the beat of her heart and the soft slither of her bedcovers. Fingers plucked at her, not quite hard enough to bruise. Tender pinches at her earlobes, her nipples, her toes. The flash of pain followed by a tiny rush of endorphins. She wanted the feeling again, again, again.

She pushed her back into a slow arch, her heels to the bed, her crown to the pillow. Again. Again. Her body was turning to something light and damp. A cloud, a wrung-out sponge. She couldn't help it: she let out a cry.

Shhhh, said a multitude of voices, sharp-edged. The hands lifted from her, her skin left throbbing, her nightdress clinging, her covers kicked aside.

They were leaving, slipping out of the crack in the window, folding back into the waves. Shhhh, said the voices as they receded, the sound of the sea inside a shell.

Ellen woke to whispers. A giggle, a thump against the wall, a laughing shush. Blinking back sleep, she opened her door and slipped into the hallway. Jenette's bedroom on one side of hers, Ash's on the other. No light under either door.

But she was sure she heard something. She stood in the hall, waiting, and couldn't shake the feeling that there was something else that she couldn't see, waiting for her to stop waiting.

She held her breath, tried to slow her heart.

Nothing, nothing.

The next morning, when Ellen fumbled downstairs, she was surprised to find that Jenette and Ash were already up. Bleary-eyed and nursing black coffees, true, but still up.

'Look at you two, all bright-eyed and keen.'

'How's your fever?' Jenette asked. 'The paracetamol is in the cupboard if you need some.'

'Why are you up so early?' Ellen turned to fill a glass with water and caught a look between Jenette and Ash that they thought she didn't see. Was it knowing? Secretive? Guilty?

No. Just the fever making her feel strange. Making her see things that weren't there.

Ellen fell asleep at the kitchen table, waking stiff-necked to a note from Jenette.

OUT FOR A DAY TRIP. BACK LATER. XXX

Ellen crept back to bed. The day felt stretched and compressed, hours pulling endless and then gone fever-fast. Light on glass bottles, sticky teaspoons left on windowsills, the curtains drawn, her head pulsing hot and cold.

She felt like if she could just get through this, could just sleep it off, then her fever would fade. Every time she thought it had left her, the shivers overwhelmed her again.

'Did you have a good day?' Ellen asked.

'It was great,' Jenette replied, eyes dreamy. 'Perfect, really. How about you?'

'Well, not perfect. But better than I was.'

'That's good. One more quiet night, maybe, and you'll be back on your feet. You just have to sleep it off.'

'It doesn't need to be quiet.' Ellen went to the cupboard and rootled through the wine bottles. 'There's plenty left. Me and you and Ash could have dinner, play some games, maybe watch a film.'

'We can't tonight, Ellen. We've been invited to the neighbours' for dinner again, same as last night.'

'You don't mean just you and Ash?'

'That's what we told them. We figured you still weren't well enough.'

'I'm not. But a couple of paracetamol, a quick nap, and I'll be fine.' Ellen stroked her fingertip down Jenette's forearm. 'Promise I won't fall asleep at the table and embarrass you.'

Jenette pulled away – not much, but enough. 'It's probably best if just Ash and I go. As a couple, you know?' Jenette rubbed at her thumbnail, base to tip, over and over.

Ellen laughed. 'A couple. Right.'

Jenette didn't look at Ellen. If she kept rubbing her thumbnail like that, she'd make it bleed.

'Jenette?'

'Come on, Ellen. This is getting silly. Let's stop pretending.'

And just like that, the house was gone. The walls, the roof, the floor: gone. The trees closed in on them, claustrophobic, seeking. The ground was black with dead leaves, the rustle of hidden insects.

'Don't pretend you didn't know,' Jenette said, and she went to put the kettle on, and her voice seemed to come from a long way away. 'I mean, God. We've been so obvious. You couldn't have missed it.'

The ground cracked apart and they both fell into the earth, down into the dark, and Ellen couldn't see anything except Jenette's eyes gleaming silver. Tree limbs scraped at her feet, her hands, her eyes.

'And you were playing up to it, Ellen, you know you were.' Jenette's laugh was high and hard. 'Flirting with me in front of Ash last night, trying to be sexy for him. You must have known what that did to him.'

'No,' Ellen says. 'No, of course. I was just–' and she smiled, down there in the dark, in the belly of the earth, and her face shattered with the force of it, and beneath it was just blood and bone, the tear of muscle, and still she smiled. 'I was just kidding.'

'Cool,' Jenette said. 'Love you.' And she kissed Ellen's cheek, and went to Ash's room to get ready.

Even after Jenette and Ash had left - laughing, leaning, tipsy already - Ellen lay in bed for a long time, feigning sleep. Finally, after midnight, when it was clear that they wouldn't be coming back for a while, Ellen got up and went to the window. She opened it wide and leaned out into the night. She held her breath.

She waited for the silvery figures to slip out of the trees and towards the cabin; waited to see the shadows they cast as they stretched out their spindly fingers up her window, their long teeth click-clacking; waited to smell the coppery, sweet-rotten scent of their magic; waited to hear a staccato crack crack crack as the borders between worlds broke and remade to let in yet more beautiful, terrible things. She knew they were always there, hidden, waiting for something they wanted.

She stayed at the window for a long time. She saw trees and stars and night. She stayed there for so long that her legs went numb and her eyes blurred with tears, and then she went to bed.

She wasn't disappointed, exactly. It would be silly to wish for danger. It would be silly to want to be taken.

My wife is not my first reader any more. She won't hear any more of the stories. She won't even let me talk about them. She hasn't heard anything I've said for a long time.

Girls are Always Hungry When all the Men are Bite-Size

T hirteen people around the table. Our hands splayed along the edge, pinkies linked. A black velvet cloth splotched with wax, itchy-slick. And candles, obviously – bloody hundreds of them, and I've had to stop using hairspray for fear my head will catch on fire. Mum would likely film it and make a mint, call it *spontaneous ghost combustion*.

Mum works so hard to set these things up. Books from the library about olden-day seances, endless internet searches to get the words right, all that shit. She makes everyone call me Eleanor now, not Ellie like when I was little. Sounds more old-fashioned, she says, more ghostly. More like a girl who would actually be haunted.

I'm at the shadowiest part of the table, my hair pinned up on my head, my dress buttoned right up my throat, my skirts tent-wide. Mum wasn't kidding about the old-fashioned look. The bigger the skirts, the more secrets live inside. She tends to go for a sluttier look, a kind of Eastern madam. Lots of kohl, lots of cleavage, lots of costume jewellery. The clink-clank of her bangles can cover a lot.

I check my hair, check my throat, check my skirts. I've done this approximately three billion times now. There's something different about this one, though, because there's a man.

I mean, there are men sometimes. Weird and old, ears hair-tufty, breath a fight between onions and cigarettes and peppermint. But not men like this. Not men that make my heart beat hard against my corset – no, really, Mum actually makes me wear a corset too. She trawls through endless vintage fairs and online auctions to find them, proper ones with laces, not zips or clips. And right now I wish she didn't, because I'm finding it hard to catch my breath.

He's not much older than me. Tousled hair, stubble, skin, all a kind of pale muddy brown. Eyes bright green, smudged under with shadows, staring at me like he's haunted.

And I could make that be true, I think, sitting there in my old-fashioned clothes in my weird tiny house about to do some minor fraud with my mother. I have that power.

*

Another dog and pony show. This one I will debunk in moments. I barely have to try any more, so predictable are their ploys. When I began I quickly filled a website with details of their scams. Now such lack of originality barely warrants a blog post. Vomited ectoplasm is strips of gauze unravelled from the cheek. Shivers and sweats are from ice or heat packs. Mysterious voices are speakers hidden in the walls. Easy to destroy this one and move on to the next. So deeply, deeply dull. The mother's name is Theo. She has black lines crayoned around her eyes and piles of clacking rings. Her breasts swell gelatinous over her tight dress. In combination with the house she is nothing but a rank mix of clichés. The tatty velvet tablecloth and bank of candles are textbook Victoriana, while she is a Halloween gypsy. And the daughter. Miss Eleanor, we're instructed to call her. Lord help me, I can't even bear to comment on that. Such an odd, languid child to have grown up in this flimsy plasterboard house. There's something of Alice in Wonderland about her. The child so clear inside the almost-woman. There are thirteen of us around the rickety dining table, and the room is so small that the backs of all our chairs touch the walls. I can't see any doors other than the one we came through from the street. The only other way out is upstairs. Is this house nothing more than a tower, a stack of tiny rooms? It might be of interest to explore, though I doubt that will be necessary. I will reach the root of this deceit. This Theo is no genius, and there are no new tricks she can teach me. Help us all, here we go. The candles are burning, the girl is in her trance, the mother is intoning commands to the spirits. My recorder is running, my eyes are open. I will find what they are hiding.

*

His eyes spark when he looks at me, like he'd like to set me on fire. I try not to smile, but I know that I've already taken up residence in his head. Oh, wait until he sees. He has no idea what lurks beneath these tight-lacings.

Mum starts her spiel about how important it is for everyone to stay in their seats with their hands splayed. They mustn't break the circle, mustn't stand or move or flee in terror. Mum says this is for their own safety among the spirits, but obviously it's so they don't see the strings and hidden things.

Under the table, I slip off my shoes. The hot guy is right opposite me. I wonder what would happen if I stretched out my leg and pressed my bare foot between his legs. Would he shake me off, stand up, storm out? Would he slip his hand into his lap and hold my foot so I couldn't do my tricks? Or would he stay still, keep his face blank, and just… let me?

But I don't do anything with my foot except what I'm meant to do, which is wait until Mum calls three times for a message from the spirits and then crack my toe joints against the floor, making the sounds echo through the laminate boards, which is easy to do because they don't have underlay. Oh, and I also have to pretend to swoon and sway in a trance. It takes some coordination to do that all at once, let me tell you. And in a corset too. I never got to go to ballet classes, but I would have nailed that shit.

I'm just getting into it, the cracking and the swooning, and Mum has got herself high as a kite, practically frothing at the mouth, demanding answers of the spirits and telling everyone that this is the most dangerous point, they mustn't break the circle, they mustn't open their eyes, they simply mustn't, oh the spirits, the spirits, their power, oh her poor dear child, and I can see through my half-open eyes that every one of the idiots around the table is really into it, faces raised and expressions ecstatic.

Except the hot guy. He's staring at me, jaw steady, barely blinking. He doesn't look angry or scared. He looks … amused. A little bored, maybe.

I feel a jolt of excitement that any second now he's going to reach down and grab my bare feet, pull my body towards him, hold me still and say: *Let's see you make those noises now.* I could make him do that; I'm the one in control here. It makes me giddy.

But he doesn't do that. Instead, something else happens, and it makes me forget to crack my toes and makes him stop looking bored and start looking intrigued.

*

To conduct a proper investigation, I must be aware at all times. When Theo instructed us to close our eyes, of course I did not comply. Such a cheap trick to hide her other cheap tricks. However, this means that I am the only one looking. So only I see that the cherries that drop to the table and roll over the velvet towards me do, in fact, manifest from thin air. They do not drop from the ceiling. They are not thrown by a hidden accomplice. They are not there, and then they are there. Before I can react, there's a sound in the walls. It comes from all sides and all at once. Moans and sighs. They sound real, not from a speaker. Then on the ceiling. The floor. The phantom breaths come faster. Well, now. This is something. Perhaps this dog does know a trick or two. Let us see where the lies end and the truth begins.

*

Is Mum doing this? She didn't tell me she was going to do this. When I glance over she looks as shocked and frightened as the rest, but then that's the face she would be doing in any case. She always got the lead in the church play as a girl. Says she's died as more saints than I've had hot dinners.

Mum must have secretly had her eyes open all along because now they're wide, staring at the random pile of cherries that's dropped from thin bloody air to roll in front of the hot guy. Cherries, for fuck's sake, and why would she do that? She already has me swoon while wearing a corset that pushes up my boobs, so this seems unnecessary.

There are noises, too, and it's not the cracking of my toes. It's like a sighing, a soft moaning, and my cheeks burn hot because, honestly, it sounds like people fucking. I can feel that everyone is pressing their hands down on the table, so hard it's vibrating.

The sex noises get faster, louder, turn to cries of joy, the sound avalanching, and I can feel the pressure building in my hands, under my feet, in my lungs, between my legs, a steady throb in the core of me, and before I know what's happening I'm on my feet and my hands are over my eyes and I'm backing away from the table, but there's nowhere to go, my back is against the wall, and a shriek is building from somewhere, so loud it hurts my ears, and when I drop my hands from my eyes to put them over my ears instead I realise it's me, the shriek is me, and my body gives one final thrum so hard I drop to my knees at the same time that the hot guy stands up from the table and steps towards me.

The sounds stop and the vibrations stop and everything – stops.

*

This was more interesting than I expected. I will come again.

*

Things calmed down a bit after everyone left. The hot guy – Luke, he's called, though I don't know if that's his real name because he hesitated at first like he had to think up something fast. Luke took the cherries with him. I think he said he wants to study them. I mean, what? They're just cherries. Ones that appeared from thin fucking air, but still.

Mum's so into it. She did the whole decent-mother thing of helping me upstairs and tucking me into bed, and I think she liked the idea of bringing me chicken soup but we only had that powdered tomato kind so she brought me that instead.

I sleep and I sleep and I sleep, and I only wake when the phone rings. I wish I had the power to make the ringing sound stop without having to pick up the phone. I know, somehow, that it's him.

*

Of course I am an entirely rational man. I do not fall for fickles and flimsies. But if I did not know better I would say the house is jinxed. The mother is an idiot and the girl is a mere pawn, so it must be the house. Something strange is happening here. I will dig out the root of it. I have paid the mother well to stay away while I explore it properly. Of course they want to hide their little tricks, but for people like that, money speaks louder than pride. The house, such as it is, seems to have been thrown up to fill a narrow alley between red-brick terraced houses, roughly 1940s-built. Most have lace curtains in the windows, while this house's front window is taken up with a blinking neon sign: PSYCHIC READINGS SEANCES REAL TRUE CLAIRVOYANCE POWERS MISS ELEANOR KNOWS ALL. Clearly neither excelled in English at school. This house is less than half the width of the others. I'd estimate its width is less than my height, though I can't say for sure as I won't be lying on the ground to check. Each floor comprises one room: sitting room on the ground floor, where the seances are held. Then kitchen and tiny bathroom above. Then a bedroom in the attic, which the mother and daughter must share. Although I am alone when I study the house, whichever room I enter I hear noise on all sides. Noises are to be expected from next-door neighbours. But what of the 'neighbours' on the ceiling or floor of the empty house? The whole place throbs and hums with energy. I began this sure that the house was the source of the trickery, but I see now that was a trick too. It must be the girl. It's always the girl. Whatever she is hiding, I shall find it, and I shall take it from her.

*

I don't want to do another seance, but Mum says that's not an option. People have already paid, and she's already spent their money. She thinks that money is the only way we're ever going to leave this nasty little house – but I know better. Control is stronger than coins.

She invites Luke. Of course she does. I think she fancies him, though she says it's just about the money. She simpers and titters and inhales more deeply when he's there, making her voice all Marilyn Monroe-breathy and her boobs swell painfully over the low neck of her dress. Luke tries to hide it but his lip curls when he looks at her; clearly the fancying only goes one way.

She seats him with much fanfare and fanciness opposite me, so he can look right at me the whole time. So he can observe everything I do.

Well, fuck that. I'm not going to do anything at all. My shoes will stay on and my mouth will stay closed.

Whatever he wants, he's not going to get it.
Whatever he thinks, I'm still in control here.

*

The mother tries to seat me opposite the girl. Nice try, but I shall not be so easily fooled. I wait until the girl is in her seat and then I pull the table towards me, its feet scraping. There's not much room to manoeuvre, but I need to see what the girl is hiding. I have requested for no other participants to be present so that I can conduct a more thorough investigation. The mother tried to bargain with me, but a handful of banknotes changed her mind. These charlatans are all the same. I stand behind the girl's chair while the candles are lit and the mother begins her woo-woo nonsense. I tell her not to bother. I may be forced to be among fools, but they will not make me one. I lean in to the girl. I can smell her: cheap sugary perfume and something underneath – fear, perhaps? Well, she should be afraid. I am going to find all her secrets and she will be thoroughly, harshly debunked. As I approach the girl, the mother stands as if to get between us, but a few more notes push her back into her seat. I know it is crude to speak with my money, but when dealing with common liars it's the only way. I hold my hand over the girl's mouth and command her to make the voice speak. I press my other hand to her chest so I will feel if she breathes in time with the voice. I brace myself against her chair so I can press my hands hard. I feel the press of her teeth, of her collarbones, the fast throb of her heart. She is a trapped rabbit. I squeeze harder.

*

His hands are big. His skin is warm. He smells of leather and green leaves.

He's so close that the tips of his hair stroke my cheek. His hands are crushing me. My head spins.

I can't breathe.

*

How is she doing this? The sounds and vibrations are back, stronger than before. I have inspected the house and nothing is hidden. I am holding her body and she is not moving. And yet the sounds are there. The whole room shakes. The moans and sighs build as before. Yet this time she cannot break the circle, cannot pull away. The sounds grow louder. The mother claps her hands over her ears. My own ears are beginning to ache, and I tighten my grip on the girl. At that moment her body convulses and she lets out a cry against my palm. Suddenly the sounds and vibrations stop. I let go of the girl and discover a new mystery. A set of handcuffs links my wrist to hers.

*

He is inside me, and I cannot get him out. I had thought that this house was the smallest space I would ever be forced inside, but I see now that wasn't true. This body, the boundaries of it: even that can be entered, forcing the truth of me down inside, smaller and deeper and dimmer.

Last time he took photographs. I can feel him looking at them, somehow; even alone in the house I feel his eyes on me, searching, disbelieving.

How would he like it? How would he like to have no power over the things happening to him? I thought that I had power over him. But I am a girl, and no one hears me when I speak.

He comes again to the house. He pushes money at Mum without counting it - though she does, of course.

He checks the walls. He checks the ceiling and floor. He checks my mouth, using a torch to examine between my cheek and teeth. He looks right down my throat, makes me say ah, makes me hold my breath, makes me gasp and cry out so he can see right inside.

He feels under my armpits and beneath my clothing and behind my knees. Lights and mirrors and probes. He has seen as much of me as it is possible to see. He makes me conduct the seance in a simple slip dress and no shoes, my arms and legs bare.

And yet: the second we begin, so do the sounds. I convulse, and choke, and retch, no matter how tightly he holds me.

He forces my mouth open and pulls the thing out: metres of lace, the sort you find on lingerie, unspooling from my throat.

Later, when I sleep, I have nightmares, rolling and sweating in that tiny bed with my mother, and the nightmares are all about him. In the dreams I point my praying hands like a diver and push them into his mouth, pushing and pushing until my entire body is inside him. I force myself awake.

But then I'm still in this house: my bed touching the walls, the sounds of strangers on every side. I think about living that way forever. Smaller and smaller and smaller.

*

I have checked the house over and over. I swear it shrinks each time I come back. That, or the girl is growing. I have examined the photos I took of her and they are unclear. Her eyes burn so that the rest of the photo seems to blur. I will take more. They will have to be clearer and closer. I will bring a spotlight. At first, when I would observe the girl after the seances, swooning and sweating in her cheap Victoriana, how small she looked. The shoddy plaster walls loomed around her. The fake mahogany chair swallowed her. There was space enough between the table and the walls for me to approach her. I could move freely and check her surroundings and her body. Yet on each subsequent visit, each recording of her shouts and shivers, the walls have seemed closer. Before long I must stand with my back touching the wall and my legs pressed full to the back of her chair. But on the next visit I cannot even shuffle into that space. I am forced to have her sit on my lap, or there would be no space for us both in that room. It's all in the name of proper inquiry. I suspect that this strange shrinking of space is another of her tricks. Perhaps I have not debunked her yet, but it's only a matter of time. She's hiding the thing inside her. I know she is. It's not in her mouth or her throat. It's not hidden in her armpits or under her thighs. She sits on my lap in her under-wear and it's so tight to her skin that I would see anything she hid and there's nothing, but there must be something. How she bedevils me. My oppressor. My tormentor. I will banish the mother with all the money I have. The source is the girl, I know, but perhaps the mother is sparking something in her. There is one more place where women hide things. For scientific thoroughness I must check there too. Probably I should not check myself. Perhaps a doctor would visit? A gynaecologist? I need someone who can open her up and thoroughly check. It's the only logical thing to do.

*

There are no candles now. No velvet. No one.

I'm alone in the house with him and I'm wearing nothing but my skin. My legs are spread and bound to the wooden chair. All my hair has been shaved off.

He's on his knees between my legs, peering inside me, his fingers hot and the heavy eye of his camera winking, and around us the walls are moaning and screaming, and he's pushing further inside me, and I know that all he wants to do is cut me open so he can see inside.

He tells me to open my mouth, and I do. I open it wider and wider and wider.

Six months ago, before all this began, I'd have thought that this man would be enough. But I am vast. He thought he could get inside me – well, tiny man, we'll just see about that. One of us is in control now, and it isn't you.

I swallow him in one go. He doesn't even touch the sides of my throat. I can't even feel him go in.

I stand up with him inside me. This man is so small, and I am so hungry. Around me, the empty house falls silent.

I turn and leave, only partly full.

Earlier on I told you that I wrote these stories on a writing retreat in Iceland. I made it seem like it was in the past and now I'm home, but in the name of being honest with you - well, I'm still here. I'm still writing.

I know I said I was here for a month, but books generally take longer than that. This one is taking much longer, anyway. I'm going to go home soon. But not yet.

Birds Fell From the Sky and Each One Spoke in Your Voice

At night, the estate was a ghost town. But no one else was there except Sidney, so he guessed he was the ghost. Sidney's house was the first one to be finished; technically, he shouldn't be living there yet. But what with the fire in his old place, there wasn't much choice. He'd thought the developers would have argued with him more, but they seemed to have run out of money to build the rest of the estate, so maybe they were just glad to have at least one house sold. Sidney had planned to move in his own stuff, but it was all rot and soot now.

He drove through the estate. The roads all started paved and reassuring, but only the one leading to his house remained so; the others were deceptive, turning to dirt partway through, leading nowhere except into the woods. He passed a half-built play-park, ground soil still in huge sealed bags. Everything unfinished, wrapped in plastic, thwacking in the wind. A fox shrieked. He reached to turn on the radio, but changed his mind.

And there was the house at last, a looming black shape against the deeper dark. He wished he'd left a light on. He parked and scooped an armful of velvet out of the back seat.

The house smelled of paint. There was a note from the decorators on the kitchen table. He'd been away for a week while they set everything up: painted door frames, tightened threshold bars, polished out fingerprints.

Sidney deposited his burden on the couch and wandered the rooms. It looked brand new, he thought, then laughed at himself. Of course it was new. Wasn't that the point? The night windows reflected Sidney back at himself. He stared at this new housemate for a moment, then looked away.

He lifted the velvet curtains from the couch and hung them from the plastic rail. They were too heavy; the rail sagged, leaving finger-widths of night at the top and sides. So flimsy, these newbuilds. He should have known it wouldn't work to mix old and new. Tomorrow he'd go and get something light and synthetic, something that crackled and couldn't be tumble-dried. He pulled down the curtains and folded them; they'd be good for the shop. Velvet curtains were definitely a thing in the 1990s. He remembered his babysitter's house had them, though of course it was actually his babysitter's parents' house as she was only sixteen. Those curtains were a burnt orange, like the insides of cheap fondants. He used to hide between them and the window, cold glass on his back and scratchy fabric on his front, the comforting claustrophobia of his own caught breath. She'd pretend to search the room for him, looking behind the flap of the video player, inside vases, up the chimney, places he couldn't possibly fit. Finally she'd whip back the curtain and scoop him up, giggling so hard he felt sick, safe and found, never really lost at all. You'd think, considering his line of work, that he'd get used to these sudden swoops of nostalgia, but they got him every time.

Sidney opened the empty cupboard under the stairs to stash the curtains, but it was unexpectedly not empty. Crouched on the floor in the middle of the cupboard was a large red dial phone. Sidney flinched, but the phone did not ring. He went to throw the curtains on top, but was then seized with a surety that the fabric would somehow catch on fire in the night. Besides, the phone looked vintage. He put the curtains in the corner and lifted the phone. The cable trailed after, hopeful. He put the phone on the hall table, plugged it in to the wall and lifted the receiver.

Silence.

Of course the line wasn't hooked up yet; he was lucky there was electricity. Ah, but they would have needed that to light the place so prospective buyers could look around. There'd be gas too, for the oven - everyone knew those estate agent tricks, baking bread and brewing coffee to make a house smell like a home. Just the thought of that made him hungry. He closed the door to the cupboard under the stairs and went to make himself some dinner, cheered by his twin, the Sidney mirroring him in the windows, following his every movement.

After dinner, Sidney channel-flicked. He got engrossed in a film before realising it was about a missing child, and quickly changed over. Then he changed it back and kept watching. It was, from his experience, unrealistic, and he found that fact strangely reassuring. The missing child was a moppet; too cute to die, but with appealingly large eyes that carried tears well. Listening to the film's dialogue, Sidney heard someone refer to the child as Cotton, and for a moment his blood stopped flowing. But he'd misheard; the name was just the sound of the mother catching a sob in her throat. His blood moved again.

Sidney watched the film to the end, even though he knew it wouldn't make any difference. The child was not called Cotton, and anyway they found him and he was still alive.

Sidney woke from the depths of night. A loud sound had just stopped. An alarm? Building site security? Thunder, hail. A fox killing something, the dying cry. In his dream, a phone had been ringing. He itched to answer it.

Sidney slid from bed, feet cold on the bare floors. Tomorrow he'd get slippers. A rug. Adult possessions. Down the stairs in the dark, the house's held breath. He didn't want to switch on the light; it would wake him up, and he'd always had trouble getting back to sleep. In the soft night he padded down the stairs.

There was the banister. There was the bottom step.

The door to the cupboard under the stairs. The hall table.

The phone.

He knew that that the phone could not have rung. Last night there had been no dial tone, and the BT engineers certainly didn't hook up phone lines at midnight. He'd made a fuss about keeping his old phone number, so he knew all about the intricacies of BT.

He knew no one had called. But he lifted the receiver. You have to answer the phone.

Silence. Of course, silence.

It was a sun-through-the-rain Monday afternoon and Sidney was just counting the pieces in a recently bought *Rugrats* jigsaw when the bell over the door jingled and the man walked into the shop. Sidney nodded politely and the man nodded back, then went to browse the Game Boy cartridges. Sidney had commissioned a special display case for them, all reclaimed wood, the shelves quarter-height so the cartridges could sit face-out but in proportion, like a doll's house bookcase; he was proud of that idea, and many a hipster had squealed ironically and asked to buy it, the whole thing, shelves and cartridges, presumably to display ironically in their ironic living rooms.

Sidney's shop sold everything he remembered from his childhood, and some things he didn't. But every single thing was from between the years 1990 and 1999. He scorned remakes, reissues, faux-vintage kitsch; in his shop, it was genuine or nothing. If you wanted a DreamPhone board game, a pink inflatable backpack, a jungle-pattern Adidas shell suit, a box of red floppy disks, platform Buffalo trainers, a Right Said Fred cassette single, Tamagotchis, Goosebumps books, a box of Cherry Coke Lip Smackers still sealed in plastic – Sidney had it. An entire childhood, both real and ideal.

Sidney observed the man without the man realising he was being observed. It was a vital shopkeeper skill, part of his arsenal against shoplifters. The more he watched, the more uneasy he felt. The man looked like a 1950s greaser, like the one in the film you're meant to think of as the bad boy – but a Hollywood bad boy, not a genuine one; borrowing cars and returning them later, maybe smoking a joint or feeling up a girl in the back seat. Leather jacket with a popped collar and wide shoulders, fastened a shade too tight over his belly, oily-looking black T-shirt, grey hair quiffed into a ducktail. There was something unwholesome about the man. He seemed stiffly relaxed, too self-conscious, like he was an actor playing a role but could easily switch into another. Sidney sensed that the man was about to look at him, and quickly glanced away.

'Looking for a Nokia,' said the man. His voice was low, as if mid-seduction. 'One of the old ones.'

'Everything I've got is old. I don't do replicas. But no phones.'

'No Nokias? I don't mind which model.'

'No phones. At all.'

'Well, are you going to get any in?'

'No. Don't do them. Don't even have a shop phone.'

'Mate.' The man paused until Sidney looked up from his jigsaw; with the bright cartoon pieces in his hand he suddenly felt ludicrous, like a child playing shops. 'You've got all this shit.' The man motioned at the Mega Drives, the floppy denim hats, the *Maid Marian* VHS, the Fisher Price extendable skates, the Cadbury's Dairy Milk dispenser, the Pogs. 'And not a single phone? Mate.'

Sidney shrugged, and felt even more like a child. He cleared his throat and felt even more ridiculous; what was he going to do next – smooth down the moustache he didn't have?

'Sorry. Too many of them around, and I like to keep things special.'

The instant Sidney said the words, he regretted them. The man's gaze raked down and up Sidney's body and his smile split wide; his teeth were straight and white. For a second Sidney thought he had a toothpick between his incisors, but he must have imagined it. He'd been watching too many films. Jesus, next he'd be expecting the guy to take off his leather jacket, unroll a pack of Lucky Strikes from his T-shirt sleeve and clack open a Zippo. Put the cigarette between his teeth. Grin wide and white. Call him a good boy.

'Special, huh?'

Sidney stood up. This had the disadvantage of revealing more of his admittedly not very lech-worthy body to the man, but at least now they were the same height; Sidney might actually have been in inch taller.

'Write your email down,' said Sidney. 'I'll let you know if anything comes in, okay?' Anything, anything to get the man out of the shop. The man leaned in – a smell of maleness, aftershave and outside air – and wrote a series of numbers on a piece of scrap paper on the counter.

'You can call me.'

'Thanks,' said Sidney, though what he meant was no.

'Thank you.' The man's wink was implied rather than literal. He opened the door and the bell jangled. Memory lurched in Sidney. He had to sit down and count the jigsaw pieces from the start before he could convince himself that the bell over the door was not the same one that had rung in his sleep last night.

When Sidney's little brother Cotton had been snatched from his babysitter's house, no one saw anything. There was no evidence. No trail to follow, breadcrumb or otherwise.

Police swarmed the house. Days of fingerprint dust and room searches and TV appeals and lists of everyone they'd ever met. Days of interviews with every neighbour and teacher and family friend. Days of badgering the tearful, apologetic babysitter, who had been in the kitchen making the boys a snack and was certain, absolutely certain that she'd locked the front door.

Cotton's face was repeated on a thousand posters, pasted on every shop door and lamp post and noticeboard. It was an appealing face, moppet-like, a face made for an easy life. His unexpected curls, his tiny cleft chin. None of it helped.

Days and days and days. Weeks and weeks. Everything, everything except for Cotton.

The police set up a tip line, and people called the station every day with information. Now it wasn't that there were no new leads. There were plenty: an avalanche, a glut. It was a small town; the police brought in officers from other towns, but there was still too much. So many helpful citizens out there, helping. Calling to share every detail they could possibly think of.

I saw a boy at the shops. He looked a few years older than the missing boy, and his hair was a different colour, but you never know what those kidnappers can do, surgery and all sorts, I wrote down the number plate so you

My cousin is acting suspicious. I tried to show him a picture of my little son but he didn't want to look. Don't you think it's strange? I think he has something to do with that missing boy

I overheard a guy walking past my house say something about a boy and a van, I didn't get his name but I drew his face, you could make posters

The next morning, Sidney opened his front door, then shivered and closed it again. Summer was definitely over, though he couldn't remember it starting. He opened the cupboard under the stairs, his mind already on the endless list of tasks that the shop seemed to bring up every day, and stared dumbly at the pile of orange velvet within.

Coat. Coat. He should have made coffee; his brain felt fuzzed, mossy. But of course his coat wasn't in the cupboard. It was upstairs, in a stack of cardboard boxes with all the rest of his clothes. He raced upstairs and dug through the boxes, then pulled on the coat. As he pounded back downstairs, without thinking he put his hand in the pocket for his car keys, which he'd left on the hall table beside the phone. He hadn't worn this coat since the previous winter, and the pockets were tiny time capsules. He pulled out a crumbling piece of gum, three receipts for pumpkin spice lattes – repulsive things they were, just the memory of the smell of them turned his stomach; he'd only bought them because the woman he was seeing at the time was inexplicably obsessed with them – a tissue hard with old snot, a small black button with a snapped thread tangled in its eyes. He put the things on the hall table and picked up his keys instead. Then he put down the keys and picked up the red receiver. It wasn't silence, he now realised. There was no dial tone, but there was something. Static. A held-breath hum. And somewhere in the distance, just under the sound of his flowing blood, when he pressed the phone hard against his ear and really listened hard, something else.

By the time he got out to the car, he knew he'd be late opening the shop. But it wasn't his fault. You have to answer the phone.

The *Rugrats* jigsaw had sold almost immediately – and at the ridiculously high price he'd put on it too, almost as a challenge to his customers, some of whom he was actually starting to resent – so Sidney was pretty happy to have found a job lot of retro jigsaws online. The downside was that counting all the pieces was a right pain in the arse. As it was a job lot, too, clearly from the same household and probably forgotten in an attic for decades, there was no way to know for sure that the pieces weren't mixed between the boxes. What if someone bought a *Teenage Mutant Hero Turtles* 1,000-piecer only to find that instead of April O'Neil's face, the only piece left was Marge Simpson's left shoe? Sidney felt life was far too short to have that conversation. So there was nothing else for it: he would have to make up each jigsaw individually, to check. All nine of them.

He had just finished making the edge of an *Aaahh!!! Real Monsters* 800-piecer, the rain was scattering a lullaby on the front window, his favourite song had just come on the shuffled playlist, and he was thinking that life wasn't such a downer after all, when the bell over the door rang and the 1950s greaser came in. He shook his lapels to get the rain off his jacket; his hair was so slick the rain didn't seem to have touched it. Sidney held the tip of his tongue between his teeth and gave the man a shut-mouth smile, then carried on with his jigsaw. He felt like he'd been tricked into a role play, but didn't know how to play something else. He knew he should collapse the jigsaw and put it back in the box. Get to his feet. Pick up a pricing gun or the credit card machine. Something adult-like. But he stayed behind the counter, head bowed, toying with a piece showing Oblina's inviting, red-painted mouth. That made him think about his ear, which still throbbed from holding the phone for so long. He hoped that wasn't red too.

Sidney looked up to steal a glance at the man, but the man was already looking at him, mouth quirked up at the side flirtatiously. He looked as if his clothes covered not a body, but something else. In the shape of a human, but not.

'You been listening?' the man said, which made it seem like he was asking Sidney if he was listening to him, but Sidney was sure he hadn't been talking. When he spoke, his face twisted and sagged, mask-like. It was age, Sidney told himself, age and wrinkles and loose skin and a flabby body. He was old. He was old. He was normal and old. 'On the phone.' The man motioned to Sidney's head. 'Your ear. Looks sore. That'll happen if you listen so hard. I bet you never thought about not answering.'

'I don't know what you ... I don't sell phones. I told you that.'

'Noble tradition, it is. Listening. Did you know that Thomas Edison tried to invent a machine that would communicate with the dead?'

'I don't–'

'He failed, of course. The dead have nothing to say. And in Italy, another guy – I forget his name – recorded mysterious voices with an old tube radio. Spent his life trying to figure out what they were saying to him. But they weren't saying much of anything, I bet. Then in Sweden, another guy recorded birdsong in the forest, but when he listened back to the recording it was his mother's voice saying: Friedrich, can you hear me?'

'I don't want–'

'Then in Latvia, another guy made over a hundred thousand recordings of the dead, including his mother. Isn't that strange? Why is it always the mother?'

The man stepped closer and Sidney couldn't help but flinch, jolting the counter so the jigsaw pieces all ticky-tacked down on to his shoes.

'Have you heard of anything like that?'

'I don't. I don't. No.'

'Still looking for that phone. Got things to say, you know?'

The man winked at Sidney. Then, incredibly, he pulled a pack of Lucky Strikes from his pocket and clacked open a Zippo. He put the cigarette between his teeth. He grinned wide and white. Don't say it don't say it please please don't call me a good–

'Call me if you hear anything,' said the man, and he lit his cigarette and opened the door and the bell jangled. Long after he was gone, Sidney could smell the smoke. His ear ached from the echo of the bell.

*

After weeks of people phoning about Cotton, the police had so many tips that dozens of them were working round the clock to investigate them all. It was too much - but nothing could be ignored. The truth was a needle in a stack of needles. The police put a special tip-line phone in Sidney's parents' kitchen, so that they could deal with the tips and the police could get on with investigating them. The phone was red and plastic, and when it rang, Sidney's parents had to answer it and write down the tips in a special folder. And when Sidney's parents were out, Sidney had to answer.

At first the tips were okay. Hearing that it wasn't a policeman's voice on the end of the phone, but a child's, people were kind. They spoke softly. Reassured him that Cotton was surely fine, surely would be home soon.

Listen, darling, I saw a man, can you write this down? He was at the supermarket and he was buying kiddie things. Little boxes of raisins and lollipops and potato waffles and chicken kievs. I bet you like those, don't you? If you can write it all down and show the policeman—

The PE teacher at the primary school is strange, don't you think he's strange? My boy forgot his kit once and the teacher made him do it in his underpants, it's just not right, it's not proper, would you play games with the other boys in your underpants?

For a while Sidney wrote all the things down in the special folder to give to the police. He wore a pack of pencils down to stubs. But the calls kept coming, all day and all night, and Sidney was almost a teenager now and his parents weren't there all the time.

I saw that boy, that missing boy. He was locked in a shed. It was my shed. If you come and look I can show you—

My dad hurts me and I don't like it and he could have hurt your brother too and at night he comes into my room—

I know why your brother got taken and you didn't. He's so little, so pretty and sweet, his cleft chin, I wanted to suck it into my mouth—

Sidney wrote it all down in the special folder. He listened and he wrote it down because someone knew about what happened to Cotton and he couldn't miss it, he couldn't miss it if Cotton or the man who took Cotton was on the other end of the phone.

I had a dream about that little missing boy. He's near water and he can't see. I think he's been blinded. There's water though, perhaps he's been drowned? Perhaps someone took him and drowned him? You should check all the water, the river, drains even, he's definitely blind and drowned—

I took him. I took Cotton and I put a gag in his mouth and he couldn't speak any more. But you can, can't you? Speak to me, little boy. Tell me about how—

When I was your age a man took me and he hurt me, I need to tell you, I think the man took that boy too, I'll tell you all the things he did to me, the things he's doing to that boy, I'll tell you all of it—

And then Sidney stopped answering the phone. It rang and he turned the TV up louder and it rang and he put his spongy orange headphones on and turned his tapes right up and it rang and his ears ached and it rang and he burned the special folder in a metal bin in the back garden and it rang and he thought of the cold glass on his back and scratchy fabric on his front and it rang and it rang and it rang.

Sidney did not answer the phone again. Cotton never came home. And Sidney knew, knew with a certainty that filled his head with a constant sickening buzz, that he had missed the one call that mattered.

The next day at the shop, Sidney didn't even pretend to make the jigsaws. He stood and waited with his fingers clutching white on the edge of the counter. He couldn't stand to look at the thing he'd bought; he'd wrapped it in layers of black bin bags to hide its shape from himself.

When the bell over the door rang, he knew it was the man. He was barely even pretending to be human now. He had the leather jacket and the greased hair and perhaps at a very quick glance he looked okay. But if you looked for more than a second, the thing inside bumped up wrongly against the inside of his skin, making strange lumps and hollows. His face shifted. When he spoke, his voice came out wet and echoing like from the bottom of a well.

'You got something for me? Something nice?'

Wordlessly, Sidney held out the package. The man smiled. His teeth were sharp and white.

'Well, now. That is nice.' The man took the package from Sidney. His nails were ragged as knives and cut straight through the bin bags. They fluttered to the floor, revealing a Nokia 3210, an original from 1999, fully charged and with one phone number saved.

Sidney kept his gaze down on the counter, not looking, the exact opposite of what he'd done when the man had taken his brother Cotton and he'd hidden behind his babysitter's orange velvet curtains and watched and done nothing, not even when the man had looked right at the gap between the curtains and said to him—

'You're a good boy, aren't you?'

'Yes,' said Sidney.

'This is our secret, isn't it?'

'Yes,' said Sidney.

Sidney closed the shop early so he wouldn't have to drive through the estate in the dark. He drove to his brand-new house, which had no ghosts and no curtains and nowhere to hide.

He opened the door to silence.

He picked up the red phone and took it into the cupboard under the stairs.

He wrapped himself in the orange velvet curtains and sat on the floor.

He waited for the phone to ring.

He picked up the red receiver.

He listened.

You have to answer the phone.

There's a nice rhythm to things here. My cabin, my studio. The shop and the pool. I feel like maybe this could be my life. I mean, why not? What have I got to go back to?

The thing is, a house is a family, a history, a body – but it's also a trap waiting to spring. It's also a lie.

The City is Full of Opportunities and Full of Dogs

She falls awake at 6 a.m. to fireworks. Or drums. Or guns. Or, more realistically, someone dragging a heavy suitcase down three flights of stairs. She knows the other residents do that just to annoy her, as they know she's in the room right by the stairwell. By the time she's awake enough to identify the sound, it's stopped.

She rolls over and tries to sleep, but there's little point: in half an hour the cleaners will come, every few minutes opening the squeaky door to the supply cupboard and letting it bang shut. She knows the cleaners think she sleeps too late – to them, anything post-dawn is wasting the day – and they're trying to wake her up on purpose.

The upside of the *corrala*, where she is staying, is that all the rooms look into a central, stone-flagged, open-roofed courtyard lined with walkways, meaning no windows to the outside street, meaning it's shady even in high summer. The downside is that every sound made in the courtyard or any of the rooms reverberates up, off the stone walls and the tiled floor, right to her room on the third level. Everything makes an echo. There's almost nothing soft or padded in the *corrala*; no carpet, no easy chair, no cushions. Her mattress is the only soft thing, and every hot night she lies between the bottom sheet and the top sheet like cheap sandwich filling, sweaty and meaty. She wants to leave the window open but it's big, and it's right on the walkway, and it's bad enough that anyone passing could look in and watch her sleeping, but they could easily climb through and be in her room. So the window stays shut, and she sweats.

She rolls out of bed, walking carefully toe-heel across the floor because she knows that even bare feet make loud thuds on the ceiling of the room below. She has another month here; best not to irritate her downstairs neighbour. In the shower she notices a mark on her upper arm, a sooty smudge like she's brushed past a dirty wall. She scrubs it off and hopes she hasn't left a mark on the sheets; she already feels bad that her hair leaves red-dye smudges on the white towels. After one month and fifteen towels, the cleaners haven't mentioned it, but she still feels the need to reassure them that it's not period blood. She knows *lo siento*, and could look up the Spanish for 'dye', 'stain' and 'hair', but the whole situation is too complicated and makes her feel tired, so she does nothing. As she dries herself, she catches a glance of her back in the mirror: it, too, has a sooty smudge, at the base of her spine, like someone has pushed her. She rubs it off with the now-pinkish towel.

On her way out she collects her meal vouchers, little blue date-stamped tickets she can exchange for her meals at a local restaurant. Today's day porter is different from yesterday's day porter, and the day porter from the day before that. She points at the tickets and says dos-zero-uno and does her best idiot-foreigner smile. The cleaners smoke cigarettes as they clean the rooms and she can smell the smoke floating down into the central courtyard. She worries about what the porters and cleaners all think about her, her bloody towels and her lack of Spanish. How they must hate her and bitch about her in the evenings over their cigarettes and *vino tinto* in the still-warm air.

Outside the *corrala*, the sky is flat and blue. She has *tostada con mantequilla* and *café con leche* perched on a stool outside the cafe. She's already too hot in her too-short dress and too-tight sandals. Everyone passing wears cardigans and jeans and boots and they don't look hot at all. They glare at her as they pass, thinking terrible and complex things about how sweaty and out of place she appears. Her coffee is strong and small and too quickly finished.

She works alone in an empty library. Before she came here, when she explained to people at home about the head librarian job, she felt the need to clarify: yes, the library is currently empty of other staff members and of potential readers, but it's also empty of books. It's her, and a mile of empty shelving. Everything is white or glass. Outside the glass, the sun is bright and white. The empty place where the books will go is lined with white shelves, the windows canted at angles to let in light but protect from direct sun the books that aren't there yet. These book-saving angles mean, unfortunately, that she is constantly on show, framed perfectly by the huge windows.

From the square outside, the sounds of music and laughter and traffic are constant. She is always aware of the people outside and how they can see inside and what they must be thinking about her. She goes about her working day in a constant state of double-think: one mind on her tasks, the other imagining how she looks to everyone watching. Sometimes she gets dizzy and feels she will tip over and shatter straight through the windows right in front of everyone.

Suspended in the centre of the empty white library is an empty glass box, which will some day house the collection of the city's most famous dead writer, whose body was never recovered after his murder. It contains special shelves: glass ones, so the books are visible from all angles. But these books aren't here yet either, so it's just empty glass shelves in a glass cube above the empty white shelves.

Several times now she has drafted an email to her bosses asking when they think the books will be delivered, or what they would like her to do in the meantime. But each time she deletes the email without sending it. If she asks them what she should be doing, then maybe they will ask her what she's been doing so far, and she will have to tell them that she has been doing nothing. Each day that passes without her asking what she's meant to be doing makes it less possible for her to ever ask.

She walks through the library, holding a clipboard to show everyone watching her through the windows that she has a purpose. She is in a silent one-woman play and the entire passing city is her audience.

She tells herself it's peaceful here in the empty library. She tells herself it's healthy to have such a developed sense of self-awareness. She tells herself over and over and over and she locks the door behind her and runs through her empty white glass-walled office and goes into the toilet, which she doesn't need to use, but which is walled in solid white with no glass so no one can see inside. She stays in there for so long that she thinks people must be wondering what she's doing in there.

She goes into her glass office and sends her bosses a report full of enthusiasm and elision that makes it seem like she has been very busy. Then she posts on all her social media accounts, where she is mostly followed by strangers; the bright lights in the library make it perfect for taking selfies. Then, while she's at it, she sends a quick and breezy mass-cc email full of exclamation marks and self-deprecating humble-brags to all her friends and family. At home, they will want to see her. She needs to stay visible.

She wakes at 6 a.m. feeling like a loud sound of fireworks or drums or guns or a suitcase has just stopped, the echo of it. In the shower she notices marks on the insides of her thighs. They're smudged, but look like they could have been handprints. She scrubs the smudges off, then has to get back into the shower again halfway through brushing her teeth when she finds the same marks on her breasts. As she scrubs at the marks she realises she is crying. Even in her distraction she makes sure to cry quietly so her downstairs neighbour doesn't hear. She gets out of the shower and stands on the tiles, dripping, rubbing at her wet face. She knows someone has been coming into her room. Someone has been coming into her room and touching her in her sleep. Before leaving her room she checks the window is barred, even though she won't be in there if someone does get inside.

All morning she wanders around the empty library with her clip-board, performing her play. At lunchtime she goes outside to eat her tortilla. She walks down a narrow white alley, the walls blinding in the sun. She coos at a dog, sitting obediently in the dry gutter as its owner fiddles with a bicycle. There are so many dogs here and they're so well behaved, rarely a lead to be seen – in fact yesterday she'd seen something so ridiculously adorable: a dog that was on a lead but holding the end of it in its mouth, walking itself.

She's about to turn down another blindingly white alley – even with her sunglasses on she has to squint, and the Spanish people rarely seem to wear sunglasses; how do they stand it, how can they see anything? – when there's a sudden cannon of barking, and she thinks nothing of it until she hears a woman screaming something in Spanish, and she looks behind her to see a cat, panicked and pinballing between four snapping and barking dogs, the cat leaping an impossible ten feet up a wall and falling behind a metal grate covering a window. A passing man, sandy-haired and freckled, speaks to her in Spanish, tries to touch her shoulder, to scoop her along with him, and she speaks nonsense English phrases at him until he leaves her alone.

The cat's owner is weeping and shouting at the dogs' owners, reaching her skinny arms between the bars, trying to pull the cat out, and for a moment it seems the cat's owner is reaching for a corpse and not a cat any more, the dogs stilled now, barks subsiding, and she can just hear a low miserable yowl under the woman's sobbing and then she's sure that the cat is alive but stiff with fright, refusing to come out. She turns down the alley and walks away in case she's wrong. The cat is still making noises of distress, so loudly she can feel it in her throat; then she realises she's making the noise herself, a low yowl, and she forces herself to stop.

She's almost at the library when a man, smiling and brown-eyed, takes gentle hold of her arm and speaks at her in Spanish, trying to lead her down the street. She smiles back and says *no gracias*, and the man still smiles and gently tugs on her arm, and she feels the sound of distress clawing its way up her throat, and when the man smiles his canine teeth overlap the others like a dog's, and she tries to pull away from him and go into the library, but then she thinks that she shouldn't let him know that she works there in case he comes in – he can, it's a public space after all, even though there's no reason for the public to go in there, nothing for them to see or do or think about except her. She stands still and looks at the paving slabs, doesn't speak or look at the man, pretends she's a statue – a particularly stupid statue that doesn't speak Spanish – until he leaves her alone. She goes inside and posts on all her social media and then emails her bosses a report. At her desk she maintains good posture – shoulders back, stomach in – for the benefit of everyone watching.

She wakes at 6 a.m. and showers redly and scrubs smudged fingerprints from around her throat and collects her blue tickets and drinks her coffee and sees some dogs and ignores a man until he leaves her alone. The sun shines through all the glass. She takes a selfie. Dogs bark. She sends a report about what she has been doing. She posts the selfie.

At lunchtime she goes into the square to eat her tortilla and watch a dance performance. It begins with five women dressed only in underpants, screaming, lit from below by red lights and from above by the white sun. It ends with the women, fully clothed now in fuzzy brown fabric that looks like dogskin, making animal noises and running in a circle.

She doesn't like the performance, and she turns away from it to look at the reassurance of the suspended glass box in the library. But the angle of the windows and the bright sun mean she can't see inside. She stands up and walks across the square to see the library from another angle. But she still can't see inside. The windows, covered in some kind of dark coating, are utterly opaque. She sees the reflected square, full of people talking and eating and walking and laughing and living. She sees herself, standing looking at herself.

She goes into the library and straight to the toilet. As she washes her hands she looks at the space above the sink, expecting a mirror, but there's nothing there. She stares at the blank white wall, letting the water flow over her hands. She stays in there for so long that she thinks people must be wondering what she's doing. Then she remembers that there's no one else in the library, and no one can see in, and no one will notice or care whether she spends her days hiding in the toilet or napping on the bookshelves or smearing the walls of the glass box with her own shit.

In her room at the *corrala*, she opens her window and lies on the bed with too many pillows propping up her head so that she doesn't fall asleep, because then someone will climb in and she won't be able to stop them.

She lies awake all night thinking about the cleaners, who are so angry to find her stained towels that they are all complaining and cursing her name right at this moment;

about all the various day porters, who are annoyed that she still can't speak Spanish and that they have to supply her meal tickets, and who are probably sitting with the cleaners right now complaining about her, but who await her arrival every day, eager to see whether her Spanish has improved even if only to later complain that it has not;

about the people who are paying her wage at the library, and will be discussing her work or lack of it in day-long meetings, scrutinising photos of her face, debating all the ways she is failing to be worth the money they pay;

about everyone at home, all the friends she has been too busy to individually email, all of whom must be trying to call her old number because she doesn't have a new Spanish number, who must be worried about her, talking about her, deciding even now who to contact to check on her;

about the dogs and the men, which endlessly follow her and only her all around the city, constantly yapping and chasing and nipping at her heels with their sharp teeth, desperate for her attention;

about the stalker coming into her room at night, who seems to only want to touch her, to feel her soft skin and hair, not to hurt her but only to be close to her;

about her downstairs neighbour, who must be able to hear her walk and cough and brush her teeth, who must be unable to sleep because of her proximity, who must be lying awake right now wondering when she will next make a sound. She thinks about going, now, to his door, tapping gently, letting him open it, letting him take her inside.

At 6 a.m. she is already awake and there is no noise. She runs down the stairs and her steps sound to her like fireworks or drums or guns or a heavy suitcase. She echoes.

After the first flight she stops. She walks down the corridor, which is almost exactly the same as the one above but with the pot plant in a different place. She knocks on the door below her room. No one answers. She peers in the window and the room is empty; the bed stripped, the desk bare. It doesn't look like anyone was ever there. She feels suddenly cold. The knowledge that she is alone, was always alone, settles on her like stones in her belly.

She leans over the stone wall and looks down into the court-yard. It is empty. She walks the square of the *corrala*, peering in every window into every empty room.

The cleaners are not there. At the empty desk, the day porter is not there, and neither is her little blue meal ticket. There are no dogs following her and no men. Her emails will bounce back unread. At home no one is waiting.

She feels weightless, smoke-like. She could turn to nothing and float up to the sky and no one would know, no one would see, no one would care. She is nothing.

She looks down at her sooty hands, at the marks she has left on herself.

It is her, always her, only her.

PART 2:
THE CHILD

'Let us not desert one another; we are an injured body.'
- Jane Austen

There's something I didn't tell you before. When my wife and I returned from our honeymoon, back to our new house, we started trying for a baby, and before long my wife got pregnant. She's pregnant as I write this, and while I'm happy and grateful and excited, I don't mind telling you that I'm also scared.

I'm scared of my wife's body.

I'm scared of the pinprick of child inside it.

I'm scared of what will happen when that child is much bigger than a pinprick and we have to get it out of her body without damaging either of them.

I'm scared of newborn babies, of holding them and cleaning them and not letting them die.

I'm scared of when it's my turn to get pregnant.

So here I am, telling you about being scared, in the hope that it will make me feel it less.

My Body Cannot Forget Your Body

First Fear:

At first I felt a swelling, a tightening of skin. I thought I must have eaten too many cream cakes, or had too much milk in my tea. I switched to skimmed and resolved to take the stairs. Every morning I lay on my bedroom floor and did a hundred sit-ups. But the less I ate, the bigger I grew.

When my belly had swollen so big I couldn't clasp my hands around it, I noticed a split in my skin. The gap was small; not even large enough to slide a coin in sideways. With a torch, I tried to look inside, but all I could see was darkness. I thought I saw something twitch, though it was too quick for me to be sure. The doctors sewed me up and told me it was tight now, it was good; I would be doing sit-ups again in no time. My skin strained against the new stitches. I was overripe fruit. I was shifting tectonic plates.

I stopped doing sit-ups for fear of ripping the cleft wider. Undressing for the shower, I sometimes caught a fleeting scent of damp earth coming from my discarded clothes where they had pressed against my belly. I told myself it must be coming from the half-open window; a split in my body would surely smell of nothing but my own self.

As the stitches stretched I saw wet purplish flesh beneath them. I went back to the doctors with my belly held in my hands, my gait unwieldy, my shoes slipping on the rain-oiled pavements. They peered inside me with pencil-sized torches and tutted. They used bigger needles and sewed the stitches as close together as they could without splitting the raw edges of my skin; the stitches started out as thick as prison bars, but they stretched thin as parcel string.

One morning, as I was stirring honey into my tea and gazing down at my swollen body, the little finger appeared. It was just the tip, down near my belly button. The finger kept curling round, the white crescent of a fingernail making long red scratches along my skin. I pushed the finger back in and tried to hold the edges of my flesh together. I could feel the nail nicking against the inside of my body as it tried to push through the gap. I couldn't hold myself together forever; when I let go the finger emerged, the nail doing its long scratches.

I went back for more stitches and more assurances: it was tight, it was good, there would be no escape. After the fifth stitching I realised that they couldn't make it stay in. I feared asking them to take it out. What would I do if they said no?

I could not do sit-ups. I could not climb stairs or drink tea or sleep. I could not go to work or see friends. I could not do anything except hold my body still and feel the scraping of the fingernails.

Maybe it wasn't trying to escape. Maybe it just wanted me to know it was there.

But oh, I know it now. I know when it grumbles through my broken sleep, when I wake to its nails scratching my flesh, when it reaches up and grabs food out of my hand. The thinner I get, the smaller its prison shrinks; but still it grabs the food, still it throws it to the ground. It tries to grow, but my skin can only stretch so far. The stitches press against its flesh, and I see the marks they leave: red lines across its shins and arms, string around roasting meat. I do not go back to get it stitched in again.

I sit in my kitchen in a tiny patch of sun, and I feel my bones pressing against the wooden chair. I sit for as long as it will let me. I think that if I can eat silently then maybe it will not realise, will not grab and throw. I think that maybe it will forget that I am even there. I think that maybe I will forget too.

My skin cannot stretch any more, and so it grows upwards into my body. I feel its elbows pressing hard against my spleen, its knees prodding at my kidneys, its eyes opening and closing on the inside of my collarbones. My heart still beats and my lungs still inflate, but only just.

Sometimes I think about snipping the stitches – snick, snack, snick, as easy as exhaling. It would tumble right out of me, my liver clutched in one bulging fist, my intestines tangled around its gasping throat, my heart still pumping between its teeth. It would choke on me as I turned inside out.

I sit on my chair, and I stare at the food I cannot eat, and I feel my bones pressing harder. I hold the scissors tight in my fist.

Second Fear:

You've heard that when you give birth, the baby can come out in a variety of forms, but there's really no need to worry about it. Whatever emerges, eventually it will all come together and make a baby. You might give birth to a quartet of mango-sized objects. Or maybe a whole big bunch of grape-sized objects (painless, but takes a while). Or, if you're unlucky, a pair of blood-orange-sized objects (which you haven't seen, but imagine is a bit of a struggle). You've heard of women delivering things like runner beans, like carrots, like kumquats. However the baby comes out, it will all be fine in the end.

Your friend Edith births five equal-sized lemons. She says it was awful, just awful, but in the post-birth photo she puts online she's wearing lipstick and her forehead isn't even shiny, so you're unconvinced. You think you'd quite like to give birth to lemons, if you can't have runner beans. You don't get a choice what grows inside you, of course, but you can still hope.

Your other friend Lucille births a poppering mess of pomegranate seeds. Her husband left her so you're there at the birth and you see the flood of wet red seeds and it seems it will go on forever. It doesn't look sore but you still don't want to give birth to pomegranate seeds. During the birth Lucille squeezes your hand so tight the bones scrape, and a month later when you visit her and the baby she's still talking about the pain. To be honest you think it's a bit overdramatic. The seeds must have hurt less coming out than they did going in.

But now it's your turn. And it's not good news.

Look down: you see the size of your bump? How big it's grown, that thing that's even bigger than the biggest melon you've ever seen? That's what you will give birth to. All in one go. Ripping, splitting, round and hard and ripe. It's unusual, yes, but then aren't you unusual? You always were, your mother would say, if she wasn't dead, if she hadn't died delivering the huge violent melon-shaped mass of you all those years ago.

Come on now, you can't put it off any longer. It's time to push. You may be unusual, but you are not special. The doctor has others after you. On the surgical tray the needle and thread lie ready.

Third Fear:

I'm lying here waiting for them to bring me the baby, and labour was fine, and the birth barely hurt, which when I think about it seems odd as that's not what I heard it would be like. The nurse comes in and clicks up my morphine and then leaves without saying anything, and that's fine too, right? Tell me it's fine.

When I was pregnant I did everything right. But the world can't stop just because you're pregnant, can it? You have to eat tinned tuna sometimes. You have to use a microwave. The yolks in those poached eggs were maybe a little bit runny but it would have been rude to send them back, wouldn't it? Someone has to change the cat litter and paint the nursery, after all, and it's not like you can ask people in the street not to smoke near you. You had to get that X-ray but it was just on your ankle, because it really was fractured badly, and they used that lead blanket and everything. Does wearing stilettos one time for a wedding count? That bath was only lukewarm; your nipples were hard and after you lay in the water for a while there were goosebumps on your arms, so it mustn't have been that hot, must it? You can't sit for too long but you can't stand for too long either and lying just means heartburn, so really, what are you supposed to do? Float weightless like a fucking astronaut?

The sheets are crisp and my milk hasn't come yet and my belly is still so huge and round; I thought as soon as the baby was out the bump would wrinkle right down like a deflating balloon but it hasn't, it's like the baby is still in there, and my eyes close and there's a warm bath rising up around me and sleep comes for me so soft and so dark.

The nurse brings me a baby with no skin and all his bones on show, his organs slipping around between his ribs, bendy and flexing to any shape, and maybe that's why I barely felt him slip out of me. The nurse brings me a baby with all his bones and hair radiation-soaked, speaking only in clicks like a Geiger counter, and every moment I hold him I get more poisoned, my skin flaking off and my hair drifting down into his glowing face. The nurse brings me a baby made of glass, tiny and perfect and smashable; a baby so tiny, so microscopic, that you'd need machines just to see; a baby with gills like a tuna fish; a baby with feet sharpened to a stiletto point; a baby made of cat shit, a baby with eyes that run out of his head like egg yolk.

I wake as the nurse comes into the room with a blanket-wrapped bundle in her arms, and from the expression on her face I know that something is wrong as she lifts her hand to show me what I have made.

Fourth Fear:

Colette and Alison were a couple and they wanted to have children. They went to the doctor, and they got the tests done, and the doctor told Colette she could go first.

Colette lay on her back on the white table and put her feet together and let her knees drop in opposite directions. The doctor opened up Colette and then took a little porcelain jug of fresh milk, white as bones and warm as blood, and, very carefully, poured every drop of the milk inside her. Afterwards Colette sat up, her cheeks rosy. Nine months later, a dozen bouncing babies popped out of her, each the size of a thumb and with perfect milky-white skin. Each baby cried *Mama, Mama* and closed its eyes when you tilted it back.

When they returned to the doctor, Colette lay on her back again and dropped her knees. The doctor took a glass bowl full of flower petals, and, with a neat pair of silver tweezers, one by one put the petals inside Colette. Nine months later, a dozen more perfect babies, and these ones even weed their nappies when you fed them with a bottle.

These babies were pretty great, but if you can make great babies then why wouldn't you make more? So back to the doctor. Next it was a selection of tiny diamonds, dropped into Colette with a set of antique sugar tongs. Nine months later only one child emerged, but what a child it was: it could speak right away with a perfect BBC Radio accent, and when it cried diamonds dropped down its cheeks.

Then, finally, it was Alison's turn. Yes, Colette's babies were perfect, but Alison wanted to make something with her body too. They went to the doctor and Alison took Colette's place on the white table. The doctor brought in the little porcelain jug of fresh milk. At first the milk looked fine, but as the doctor carried it over, Alison saw it turn greenish and bubbling. But the doctor knew best, so she kept her feet together and her knees dropped. The doctor opened her up, and every drop of the sour, stinking milk went inside her. Nine months later, she gave birth to a bundle of matted, oily hair. The child needed to be fed and changed and bathed, and Alison and Colette did these tasks just as they had for their other children, but it never became less oily or less matted.

They went back to the doctor and Alison dropped her knees. The doctor took a plastic tub full of serrated animal teeth, and, using a large pair of pliers, inserted them inside Alison one by one. Nine months later, she gave birth to a damp cloth that seemed to have been chewed by a dog.

They tried one more time. When the doctor approached Alison with a tin tray full of rancid purple livers and lifted a pair of rusty surgical tongs, she tried not to be angry.

She asked the doctor: Why are my children so different to my wife's?

Because, said the doctor.

She tried again: Could we try me with the flower petals? Why can't I have diamonds?

Because, said the doctor.

And Alison dropped her knees, and the livers went inside her, and nine months later another horrific malformed thing came out, except that this one looked more like Alison than any of the others. They didn't try again.

As the children grew, Colette couldn't help wondering: could Alison love her own horrid, hunched children as much as Colette's perfect, peachy, poreless ones?

The truth was, Alison did not love the children. Not plural. She loved only one: the last child, the horrific malformed thing that looked just like her.

Stranger Blood is Sweeter

Sarah knows she's been fighting or fucking or eating something. Someone.

'Fell,' Juno says, not even trying to hide it, half smiling
with a chipped canine and her left cheek bruised high and deep.
She tucks her hands under the breakfast table, away from the
unforgiving sunlight. Last week one of her fingers was broken, and
she wouldn't say why.

'You were fine when we went to bed.'

'Got up in the night to pee. And fell.'

Sarah says nothing as she puts ointment on Juno's cheek. Not
much she can do about the tooth; she's not a dentist.

Everything is fine for a few mornings – no new bruises, at least –
then Sarah wakes to a bloody pillow.

'Juno!' she says. 'What the hell?'

'Huh? What?' Juno jolts awake, the blood down her jaw crumbling dry.

'Your ear,' Sarah says.

'Oh.' Juno scratches at the blood flakes with her fingernail
and they watch bits flutter to the sheets. 'I fell and I forgot
about it.'

Sarah dabs at Juno with a damp washcloth. It looks like her ear was pulled down and released, and the very top has ripped away from her head. Once the blood's cleaned off, it's not that bad.

'You should probably have stitches,' Sarah says.

'Can you tape it or something?'

Sarah does her best, then puts away the first-aid kit. She should ask, she knows she should, but she's scared to hear the answer. She's spent years trying to figure out the damage in Juno. She knows it was something – a terrible thing, a darkness that Juno hints at but never explains. She lets her wife have her secrets. Whatever the darkness, Sarah tells herself, it doesn't make them love each other any less. But can you really love someone you don't know?

The next night, Sarah follows Juno.

The place is walking distance, but it's late and the street is badly lit and the whole time in her head Sarah's self-defence teacher is shouting: Don't walk alone at night! Keys between your fingers! Go for the eyes and the throat! Sarah pulls her scarf up over her jaw and tries to walk silently.

In the bleaching street light she sees Juno, all in black with her fists wrapped in white, disappear into a building she's never noticed before. It looks like a garage or a workshop. It's something harmless. It must be. Secret mechanic training? Extreme metalworking? Stuntwoman training. Roller derby.

Sarah leans against the wall outside, taking deep breaths, getting ready. Though the door is ajar, she can't hear anything from inside the building. She keeps her keys in her clenched fists.

She goes inside. The building is lit with red emergency lighting. She follows the narrow corridor. She strains her ears but there's nothing; only a pressure, a held breath. The definite sense of people waiting just around the corner. She emerges into a larger space and the backs of two dozen women looking down at something.

A bell rings. Two staggered thumps, like dropped sandbags. Then a wet thud, a fast exhalation. Sarah smells blood. She sidles through the massed women without looking at any of their faces, not daring to see if any of them is Juno. She comes up short on the lip of a circular pit about eight feet deep. Dirt floor. Bare brick walls.

In the pit two women circle one another, fists raised, knees bent, swaying low. One is holding her left hand oddly, as if the fingers are broken. The other has a lipstick-red smear of blood from her nostrils to her chin.

One feints, the bird-fast dart of a head, but the other doesn't fall for it. A fist below the ribs and she folds, broken hand scuffing the dirt. A kick to the belly, to the shins. She lifts her knees to protect her body. Sarah closes her eyes. The smack of flesh. The sharp smell of blood.

She pushes her way outside and vomits against the wall.

She runs away before Juno can see her. In the shadows, on the way home, she does what she needs to do.

When Juno gets home, Sarah rolls over as if she's just woken up.

'Hey,' she says.

'Hey,' Juno says, 'just went to the loo,' and this is surely the stupidest lie yet as her skin is night-time-cold and she's barely caught her breath.

In the darkness, Sarah reaches for her, pushes her hands down, down. Sarah's already wet against Juno's fingers, but it might just be blood.

Sarah stands at the sink and washes the breakfast dishes, looking at the cluster of trees that hides their neighbour's windows. Even in the morning sun, beneath the trees it's all shadow. If she keeps her hands in the water, Juno won't see what's caught under her nails.

'At work the other day we were talking about our favourite stories from when we were kids.' Sarah knows it's clunky and horrible but can't think how else to ask. 'What was your favourite story when you were little?'

'Have you seen my other work bra?' Juno's piling things into her bag, chewing a toast crust. 'The wire's coming out of this one.'

'I don't know that story.'

'What?'

'I said,' Sarah says, turning from the sink, 'what was your favourite—'

'I heard you, Sarah. I don't know, Chicken Little or E.T. or something. Hansel and Gretel, maybe? I liked the gingerbread house. Now can you please tell me if you've seen my bra?'

Sarah dries off and keeps the tea towel in her hands as she goes to find the bra, which is in the dirty washing basket where Juno left it. The problem is that Chicken Little and E.T. and Hansel and Gretel all suggest very different things. If she liked Chicken Little, then she tried to tell someone that a bad thing had happened and they didn't believe her. If it was E.T., then a friend was mistreated and she couldn't save them. Hansel and Gretel was the worst of all. Abandoned children and evil mothers and the threat of being eaten, of wanting to eat things you shouldn't eat. There are a few things that Juno doesn't know about Sarah, that she never thinks to ask, and one that Sarah will never tell is that her own favourite story was always Hansel and Gretel. When she first heard it, it made her want to eat. It still does.

She goes back into the kitchen and hands Juno the bra.

'I can't wear this, Sarah. It's dirty.'

'Why Hansel and Gretel?' Sarah asks. 'Are you hungry? Do you want more breakfast?'

'Never mind, I'll just wear the one I've got on.' Juno gives Sarah a distracted kiss and grabs her car keys. 'Later, okay? I'll get dinner.'

But later is no good. She needs to know now. She needs to figure out the appeal of the place where Juno goes. The desire, the goad. It's dizzy and sick and confused, and where is all this coming from? Who is she, really?

That night, she follows Juno again. Just walking into the place – the red light, the waiting breath – all the blood drops from her brain and her heart thuds in her throat.

She pulls her hood low around her face and elbows her way through the women to the front, toes right on the edge of the pit. The bell rings.

She watches Juno drop down into the pit. Another woman follows, dreadlocks knotted on top of her head. She raises her fists and Juno lunges, gets in a hit. The woman backs away, shakes her head, drops of blood from her nose dripping to the dirt. Juno bounces back on the balls of her feet, fists protecting her face, elbows protecting her body. The woman kicks out and sweeps Juno's feet from under her. Juno thuds to the ground but lashes out with her feet as she falls and gets the woman in the lower belly and she doubles over and reaches for Juno's hair, slams her head against the ground. Juno's got her fingers in the crook of the woman's elbow and she's pulling, trying to get free, and she lurches up and smacks the underside of the woman's chin with the crown of her head. Someone shouts, they separate, they circle one another with their hands up and their bodies low and their breath fast and hot.

The air is heavy with strangers' skin and the smell of blood and the light catches the gleam of eyes and flesh slaps and bodies thud and it's red and black and red and black and red.

The next morning she puts arnica cream on Juno's bruised forearms, she sticks butterfly stitches to Juno's split lip, she splints Juno's fractured toe.

'Clumsy,' Sarah says, 'you're so clumsy, my love.'

Keeping her mouth closed so Juno won't taste what's caught between her teeth, she kisses the broken parts, one by one by one.

The next week, Juno is away for work, and the first night Sarah lies awake in their cold bed. The second night she goes out into the shadows and does what she needs to do. The third night, she goes to the red-lit building and stands at the lip of the pit, watching.

Women punch each other in the face. Women break one another's fingers. Women get pinned to the ground with knees on their throats and retch in the dirt. Women take punches, have their heads snap back against the wall, and are knocked unconscious. Women come away with strands of each other's hair in their fists. One woman forces another into a corner and braces her hands on the wall and kicks the woman in the belly over and over and over.

When Juno gets home, Sarah says: 'I followed you.'

Juno, confused, not sure whether it's a joke. 'On my work trip?'

'No. At night.'

A long pause. 'When?'

'Does it matter?'

'I didn't—'

'Don't lie, Juno.'

'It's not a big deal. It's just – it helps.'

'Helps with what?'

'You know what,' Juno says.

'You like to beat women up?'

'It's not like that.'

'So you like them to beat you up? Do you want me to beat you up?'

'Jesus Christ. I knew you wouldn't understand.'

'Would you – can you stop?'

'I can't, Sarah. I need it.'

'Can you take a break?'

'If you know I need it, why would you ask me to stop?'

'Because I don't want to see it again.'

'So don't follow me.'

'Please. Until I get to know this new version of you. We can't be strangers. Please, Juno.'

'Okay,' Juno says. 'Okay.' And as she pulls Sarah close and kisses her, Sarah tastes the blood from Juno's split lip. Sarah kisses harder.

That night Sarah makes spag bol, and they eat it with a bottle of red wine in front of the TV, mopping up the sauce with garlic bread. The whole evening, it's nice. It's clean. It's gentle. No smell of blood, no smack of flesh.

Later they make love, and that's nice and clean too. Sarah is the little spoon, and holds Juno's arm around her tight, but not too tight. Nice. Clean.

Juno waits until she thinks Sarah is asleep, then she slips out of bed and wraps her fists and goes out alone.

Sarah hears the front door click shut and counts to a hundred. She goes out into the shadows and she finds the thing she wants. She fights it. And she fucks it. And she eats it.

I'm still in Iceland. I know I'm over halfway through this book now, and I'm really dragging it out, but I have a good reason. This will be my last retreat for a long time. There's a baby coming, and I won't be able to bugger off to the beautiful frozen north to spend weeks and weeks alone any more, at least not for a few years.

When the baby comes, I don't know how I will find a balance between my work - that swooping, strange, isolated place where ideas come from - and the everyday, slouchy, cosy, boring, sometimes claustrophobic necessities of home.

Already I worry that, at the times when I inevitably have to choose home over work, I will resent it. I worry that I won't be able to - won't want to - make space for this child, despite how desperately I want it. What if I get everything I want, and I don't want it any more?

Good Good Good,
Nice Nice Nice

S abrina leans over the net-cage and dips her long-handled scoop into the water. Carefully. Very carefully. The sharks are long gone, but still. The pods somersault in the water, tumbling oily, black as a winter night. Most are still too small but a few are skull-size, fat as puppies.

Mermaid's purses, they used to call them, back when Sabrina was small, back when they were just useless high-tide flotsam, though her mother insisted on calling them devil's purses, to Sabrina's annoyance. Sabrina never uses old-fashioned words like that at the farm; she's from the town, she's not a bumpkin. It's strange to think that the mermaid's purses used to wash up on the shore here; Sabrina never knew that there were sharks in the water. Then again, there are lots of things in the sea that we don't know about.

She shifts her grip on the scoop, keeps birling the pods, searching for the biggest. There's one ready, she knows it. The seawater splits, pulses, and there it is: swollen huge, not ink-black like the others but pink-grey, flesh visible where the collagen stretches taut. Sabrina hunkers on the edge of the net-cage and eases the pod into the belly of the scoop, lifting it out of the water. Her arm muscles shudder.

She should ring the bell, she knows; get someone else out here to help. Harvesting is a two-person job. But though the war's been over for two years they're still deep in the clean-up there, meaning they're still short of workers here. It's not ideal, but when is it ever? She braces the scoop with one hand and reaches for the harvesting kit with the other.

Squatting, she tips the pod into her lap and finds the scalpel. She breathes deep, slows her heart, gives her hands over to routine. She slips the edge of the scalpel into the rubbery edge of the pod and feels it split. The insides squirm. She waits for calm and cuts further. The pod splits, births the pink wriggle into her lap. She checks its nose and mouth – clear – its genitalia – male – his toes and fingers – ten of each. He is wailing now, perfectly. He is doing everything perfectly. All of him flawless, more perfect than a real baby could ever be. There is nothing wrong with him, now or ever. His tiny tongue. His pink gums. His curled toes. He is screaming so hard his whole body shakes.

'Hush,' says Sabrina, 'hush, you, my wee one,' and she scoops up seawater to rinse off the rubbery flecks still stuck to his skin, then dries him with a towel and swaddles him in a knitted blanket. She doesn't like to touch the empty pod, black and rubbery like a pair of abandoned galoshes; she wants to leave it there on the walkway, but the birds will come for it, and they must be kept away from the net-cages at all costs. She glances around and kicks the empty pod back into the water.

Sabrina realises she's been humming a lullaby and the baby has stopped crying. His tiny fists clench. She rubs the blanket over his limbs to warm them as she walks. She carries him in the crook of her arm, her careful steps on the rain-damp walkway, into the main farm building. The baby will be warmed, tested, named, assigned. Some day he will be a soldier, but first he can be a child. She closes the door behind her.

Outside, from shore to horizon, the net-cages stretch, hundreds of them, containing thousands of pods. Inside each one is a baby, growing, waiting.

All the way home Sabrina can feel the weight of the thing in her pocket. She's sure that people will know, will see it pulling her coat askew. Well, so what if they can see? It could be a purse of coins. It could be a make-up case. It could be a brick. She keeps a tight hold of the bus's metal rail. The town unspools past the window. The red-roofed houses, all different heights, foundations subsiding, higgledy-piggledy like a mouth of uneven teeth. The spindly stretch of the pier with the spinning carousel at its end, fairy lights strung from posts, bringing down constellations for strolling lovers. The painted-out street signs and shop names, the raised arm of the church steeple. And around it all the encircling sea, black as tar under the evening sky.

She rings the bell for her stop, nods a thanks to the bus driver. She pauses on the garden path, her hand on the gatepost. Even from out here she can hear Jamie's cries. She's become so attuned to them in the past ten months, she can interpret them like language. The screams are stuttering, gaspy; he's nearing the end of a jag. He cries and cries and cries and the only time he stops is when he cries himself into exhaustion. Then he's silent and unconscious, but it can't be called sleep. Her hand clenches on the gatepost. She makes herself let go, and when she turns the doorknob she can't feel it, her hand trembling numb.

'I'm home!' she calls, pointlessly, as everything is Jamie's snuffling cries and her mother's soothing murmur. From the radio in the kitchen, the low-high-low toot of horns, a tsh-tsh cymbal, the steady foot-tap of the drum. She turns up the volume, switches on the hob, tips in soup for two.

'I'm making supper,' she calls through, and there's no pause in her mother's lullabies, the soothe of her words so familiar to Sabrina from her own childhood. She hadn't thought it was anything special at the time, but now she'd give anything for Jamie to have a childhood like that. Floured hands shaping loaves. Thumbnail-sewing daisy-chain stems. Dooking for apples at Halloween. Even for a month. A day. A moment without pain. She would give him everything, but she can't give him anything at all.

Soon Jamie will scream himself unconscious and the soup will get eaten and Jamie will wake up screaming and Sabrina will hold him all night, every way she can think, trying everything even though she's tried it all a hundred times.

She shouldn't give him a spoon of whisky. She really shouldn't. But he won't take her milk, he won't take her comfort. What else does she have to give him? Her gaze slides to her coat, hung by the door. She drags it back and stirs the soup.

It's a sleepless night. After a teaspoon of whisky Jamie drifts – not asleep, but not quite awake, blessedly silent. Along with the whisky Sabrina feeds him the tiny kidney she stole from the organ net-cage, praying that he won't choke on it. She holds her breath as he arches his back and struggles, mewling, but it slips down. He lies quietly in her arms, and for that moment she is at rest too. Perhaps for a moment she even falls asleep. At least, she dreams. She sees the kidney grafting itself into Jamie's tiny insides, the purplish mass of it absorbing the red-raw damage in him. Of course it was the kidney all along. How silly that none of the doctors figured that out. Of course a mother knows what's best for her child.

A few hours later, Jamie wakes screaming. Sabrina coddles him, bounces him, makes soothing sounds to tamp down her despair. She should have known the kidney wouldn't work. The ear didn't work. The eye didn't work. The spleen and the liver and the snipped length of intestine didn't work. The problem isn't that he's missing these things; and even if he were, swallowing them wouldn't help. Once, weeks ago now, she spent a few heart-thump minutes touching the kitchen knives, choosing which would be best, but then Jamie woke crying for her and she slammed the drawer and never thought of doing that again.

When the sun comes through the window Sabrina's mother comes through the door. Sabrina hands Jamie over in a brief moment of quiet. He's awake but not screaming. His face blood-red, his eyes swollen almost shut, his tiny fists shaking. He looks shocked, confused, like he can't quite believe that the world would betray him this way. He's never known what it's like to not be in pain, and no one can tell Sabrina why. Something in her baby is broken, and she does not know how to fix it.

In the staffroom Sabrina rubs her eyes and drains her second cup of tea. One sugar isn't enough, but Teresa is there and she doesn't want to add any more. It's not easy to come by, the same as just about everything else these days. Nothing comes easily; nothing can be wasted.

Teresa sneers as she drinks her tea. The tea isn't the problem, although it tastes of sawdust and the milk is powdered. Teresa doesn't like working at the farm. She thinks it's unnatural, raising these shark-babies as if they're human babies. Teresa is an idiot. They are human babies, can't she see that? Realer than real. There's not a bit of shark to them. Just because they're grown in the pods. Teresa has three sharp-smiled boys of her own, each taller than the doorway though the oldest is barely twenty. If there's a bit of the shark to anyone around here, it's Teresa's oldest.

Sabrina is proud to work at the farm. She was proud when it was a salmon farm, but that's nothing compared to how she feels now. When the farm first switched over, she'd tried to learn about every aspect. Her job is just the harvesting, but she wanted to know all of it, how every stage works. That was before Jamie, right enough; now she has no space in her head for anything outside him.

The story goes that a child, some ragamuffin beachcomber, split open a mermaid's purse with his toy penknife, then ran home squawking when a cluster of human teeth tumbled out onto the sand. Perfect, they were: ready to be transplanted into any raw gum. And they took, and they held. You'd never even know. For a while they just took the teeth as they were given, but there were so few, and no real system for finding them.

That scarcity makes sense now that we know you don't get something from nothing; the teeth didn't just appear, did they? Remnants of shipwrecked sailors, maybe, or people murdered and dumped at sea, or natural deaths whose families were too destitute to buy a burial plot. What mattered is that some teeth went in, and some teeth came back out – and they were perfect, better than the ones our own bodies grow. The same for kidneys, lungs, ovaries.

Ah, and who made the sharks that made the parts? Who put them there in the waters around the Scottish coast? Well, best not to ask. Sabrina's mother used to caution against looking gift horses in the mouth. A war hangover, the best of a bad situation. The folk of the town always were good at that.

But what will they do if another war comes? Sabrina feels sick to think of these perfect babies shipping off in subs and battle-ships, off to die so she can live. Are they really less real than she is? Than Teresa? Than Jamie?

The memory of predawn screams makes Sabrina's headache flare. She's let her third cup of tea get cold. It doesn't matter; it didn't have sugar in anyway. She tips it in the sink and goes out to the net-cages.

Jamie screams all night. Sabrina holds him tight to her body, his siren mouth right by her ear, shushing and soothing him for so long that her lips go numb.

The next day, Teresa is off sick. Sabrina covers for her in the nursery. The oldest baby there is only weeks old, as they don't stay there long. Plenty of women are keen to take them on as their own. So many sons and husbands lost to the war, so many empty homes and hearts. So far the babies all live in this town; it's not a secret project, exactly, but it's not openly discussed. They just let the babies get a little older, grow into children and then adults, just to check that everything is working well. Perhaps one day there will be a farm like this in every coastal town. Sabrina's heart drops at that thought, which makes no sense. She shakes her head at herself – such ridiculousness! She must be tired. This farm, the babies: all of it, nothing short of a miracle.

It's quiet in the nursery. Sabrina warms bottles and launders socks to the sounds of the babies' quick clear breathing, the shuffle of their kicking feet, the occasional giggle and gurgle. Should babies be able to giggle at a few days old? She doesn't think she has ever heard Jamie giggle. Perhaps he never will. Grief chokes her, and she turns back to the bottles before the babies see.

When the bottles are ready, she starts the first feeding. She scoops the baby into her arms, nestles him into the crook. He blinks his baby-blues at her and smiles and grasps her thumb. Can babies smile at that age? Can they grip that hard? All of a sudden she remembers Teresa, her tight lips as she makes her tea, her steady frown.

Sabrina nudges the bottle's nipple to the baby's mouth. He takes it right away, tiny mouth suckling, tiny throat gulping. He reaches up his hands and holds the bottle, takes the weight of it – but that's ridiculous; he hasn't, he can't.

Sabrina releases the weight of the bottle slightly and it drops, of course it does, and the milk all tips to the base and the baby is sucking at nothing. She tips it back and he keeps drinking, his tiny hands waving, reaching instinctively for the bottle that he most definitely can't hold. Sabrina settles into the feeding chair, nestling the baby into her, relaxing in. Those early days and nights with Jamie: perhaps this is what it was meant to be like. The warm weight of the tiny animal, the snuffly breathing, the shared contentment.

Something is wrong. Sabrina sits up. She checks the bottle, the breathing. The baby's eyes are bright. The baby's lungs are clear. The baby is feeding fine. But still, she knows that there is something wrong. She thinks she understands now why Teresa says the things that she says.

She looks down at the baby, his trusting gaze, the perfection of him.

Teresa is an idiot. They're not sharks. They're babies, just like any other babies, but better.

If they look like babies and act like babies and grow like babies, then what else are they?

On the bus home, her pockets are empty. She tries to imagine what Jamie's giggle would sound like, but she can't.

Jamie screams all night. Sabrina knows she must have slept at some point in the ten months since he was born. She must have, or she would be dead. But it's hard to remember what it was like.

She spoons a little whisky into his screeching maw and that helps a little. She wants to hate him. It would be easier. But she loves him completely. She would give him any part of her body if she thought it would help. She would scoop out her eyes, scissor off her toes, burn off her breasts, smile and coo at him as she bled to death if it would stop his pain.

But she sees now that it's not what's inside Jamie that is wrong. It's what Jamie was inside of. It was her. She was never meant to be a mother. All she can give him now is a better start; another mother.

Sabrina goes out in the night. Her arms are heavy with their burden. The sleeping town unspools past her as she walks, and then she runs.

She stands at the edge of the net-cage with her baby in her arms. His stuttering cries are so high her eardrums ache. His fists are the softest things she's ever felt. They clench and unclench along with her heart.

At her feet, an empty mermaid's purse is open, waiting. The water boils with dozens of perfect babies waiting to be born.

This part of Iceland is quiet, but it's not completely empty. It's not like it's just a huge iceberg and then me.

There's the cabin where I sleep and eat. There's the window-lined studio where I write. There's a road where the odd car passes. There's a field with horses in it. There's a shop and an outdoor swimming pool. There are houses. There are people, sometimes, though rarely, and when I do see them I can't say much as I don't speak a single word of Icelandic, to the point that I can barely pronounce the name of the town, and I feel stupid about it, about being an ignorant monolingual English speaker.

My favourite thing here is the outdoor pool. Every evening I swim. A hundred laps, slow and steady, pacing my breath. By the time I get out my legs are shaking, my head spinning. I don't feel quite myself. I feel like I'm in a dream world. Like anything could happen.

The Only Time I Think of You is All the Time

It was hard for Brigitte to get to me at first. She'd push against the barrier for hours, getting more and more frustrated at me for not being able to see her or hear her. When she finally appeared to me, waking me in the night, she'd have been talking for so long with no one listening that the words had turned to slush and mutter. Before Brigitte, I woke calmly, to the morning sun or birdsong or the natural end of my dreams. Now it's a sudden fall awake, her hands gripping my shoulders, her face right up close to mine. Her constant tumble of words, an avalanche of scree, falling out in a low mumble, steady as earth.

I know how Brigitte died. She drowned. I don't know if it was an accident, or she did it to herself, or someone else did it to her. But I know she drowned because she was underwater for so long that her eyes turned milky, and they still look like that now. In our after-lives we'll all look the way we did at the moment of death, I guess. It's strange to see her in water; I feel like I should try to save her from it, keep her dry and breathing, though it's far too late for that.

It's hard to remember now what baths used to be like. The book, the bubbles, the fizzing glass: it's like something I saw in a film once. Now Brigitte climbs in after me and chatters in my ear. Once I lost patience and tried to hold her under, just for a moment of silence. But she just laughed at me and then there was a hell of a mess with the water on the floor and I'm the only one who can clean it up, after all.

I don't know who Brigitte is. Who she was. She seems to be – to have been – in her late thirties, early forties. She has long brown hair and small hands. Her face is bloated from the water and I can't tell what colour her eyes were, but I'm sure I never met her. She wears a nightgown, ankle-length and white and always drifting around like she's falling in slow motion, but it's a timeless design so it's hard to place it. I think she might be from a long time ago. Decades or centuries, many generations. Perhaps it takes a really, really long time to work your way back to here from wherever you go. I don't know who she is and I don't know what she wants, other than to be near me and talk to me always. What kind of monster am I for resenting that? For resenting a love so obsessive, so all-encompassing, so perfect? Most people go their whole lives without being loved like that. I should appreciate it.

She can come to me whenever she wants to, and what she wants is all the time. If I'm asleep or distracted or trying to do something, it's harder for her to get my attention. Her words are still there but I've stopped hearing them. That's when she gets frustrated. I work from home now; it wasn't a good look for me to suddenly respond to her in the middle of a meeting or while on the phone. I still don't know whether other people could see her and were frightened at the sight, or if they couldn't see her and were shocked by me suddenly shouting *shut up shut up please for fuck's sake shut up* at nothing. I don't know how you ask people something like that.

I still live in the house I grew up in with my mother, which is also the house my mother grew up in with her mother. They're both dead, so it's my house now. I had a wonderful childhood here. My mother and I loved each other so much; it was just the two of us, a tiny team, together all the time. My grandmother died when my mother was small so I never met her. My mother died when I was small too. I miss them both. I know it might not make sense that I miss my grandmother when I never met her, but I do. I miss how much I would have loved her.

There's only one place I can go where Brigitte can't find me. Behind the house is a long, rambling, overgrown garden, and at the end of the garden is a pond. On top of the pond is a layer of algae, summer-stinking, blanketing the black water. Over it hums a constant shift of black flies. There is nowhere now that she is not – nowhere except here. I have to make sure she won't find me. It's not enough to just be beside the pond. I slide into the water, feeling the wet algae slime up my calves, my thighs, my belly, my breasts, my throat. Under the water, invisible things squirm. The water is the colour of stewed tea. I close my eyes and take a big breath and dip my head under the water. Silence. Darkness. I feel my heartbeat pulse in my ears. The water presses on my eyes. I am alone, finally alone, if only for the length of a breath.

I know I shouldn't go to the pond so often. She will get suspicious. I know she will eventually find me here, and every time under the water is a new risk. But the constancy of her. It drowns me. Here under the algae in the stale water, I have peace. Insects flick along my arms. Weeds tangle around my ankles. I know it's ridiculous to feel so suffocated by her. It should be nice. Comforting. A middle-aged woman watching over me, keeping me company. It's not like she's got yellowed claws or black eyes that drip blood. It's not like she hides in corners facing the wall or cackles at strange moments or runs her talons through my hair as I'm washing it. She's just - there. Wherever I go, whatever I do. I walk down the street and I feel her toes stepping on the backs of my heels. I type emails and I feel her fingers on top of mine. I read a book and she bends the cover back so she can read it too. I get in the bath and I see the water rise as she climbs in after me. I go to the toilet and she slides her fingers under the door, calling my name. The constant presence and noise of her. She chatters, chatters, chatters, day and night, never pausing for breath because she doesn't have to breathe. Her voice fills my head until there's no space for anything else. I've been under the water too long, but I'm not ready to come out. I know, I just know, that she has found me. If I surface, there she will be, ready to reach for me: to stroke my face, to kiss my cheek, to twine her hand in mine. Wanting me, needing me. Bright lights flash inside my eyes. My heart throbs. Just one more second, please. Just one more moment of space and silence. I press my hands hard against the walls of the pond to hold myself under. I think of my mother, and how much I loved her as a child - obsessively, all-encompassingly, perfectly - and how much I love her still, even after she drowned in the pond.

We Can Make Something Grow Between the Mushrooms and the Snow

The Mushroom House

Eco-friendly and ripe for development, this highly unusual dwelling will make the perfect home for the right occupants. Buyer, be aware that house is set on a bed of mushrooms with most of the organism below the soil surface, providing a sturdy and constantly growing base for the structure. The organism's above-surface aspect forms the walls and roof. Three public rooms, two bedrooms, family bathroom – though these will expand as the organism grows. Damp proofing recommended.

Richard's notes: Three seconds in this house, and I feel my body pulse fertile as earth. It's perfection. We can have children here, I know it. Three, four – eight, ten. As many as we want, no effort at all. What can I say? It's a house made of sodding mushrooms, and I bloody well love it! I really can't see a single problem. Where can I sign?

Carolyn's notes: This is not a house. It's a pit of rot. The walls are grey and spongy and everything stinks of decomposition. My feet are mired in dirt. Every time I breathe I feel like I'm inhaling spores, invisible things that will wriggle and burrow and grow inside me. I could never work in a place like this. I need space and quiet, cold and clarity. This grimy, mildewed house is the opposite of that. How quickly can I leave?

The Bluebell House

This charming and unique cottage is situated in the centre of a blue-bell wood. Previous owner was a witch, but house has been profes-sionally cleaned with bleach and appropriate rituals. Bijou, but still with all the necessities. Big enough for a family, assuming the family is one person, or multiple people who are very small. Living room, two bedrooms, outdoor bathroom. Good-sized kitchen, particularly the oven.

Richard's notes: Carolyn wouldn't take the mushroom house, even though she got pregnant right after we went there – I knew it was a fertile place! I'd happily have stayed there. But hey, marriage is about compromise. It's creepy to me that a witch lived here. Cast her weird spells and curses, thought her nasty thoughts. For all we know, she cooked stolen children in that oven. The estate agent didn't say that, but I've read the stories. Still, perhaps bringing a child here would be a good thing. Perhaps it would cleanse it. I mean, we're certainly not going to put any children in the oven! I think we could make a good go of it here.

Carolyn's notes: The flowers on the ground here are thick as dust. The second I got near the house, I was choking on pollen. But I'm trying. I even brought my research books with me to see if I could do some work, just as a test. He goes on whether or not he likes the place, but for me it's more complicated than that. If I can't work, I can't earn, and we'll lose whatever house we're in. I left him talking to the estate agent and tried to work. Nothing came. I can't think. Can't breathe. The pollen is inside me.

The Cave House

Sturdy roof and walls. Open aspect to the front, interior fully open-plan. Easily maintained. Free food and water sources in the form of lichens, mosses and a nearby stream. A fixer-upper, ideal for an enthusiastic and motivated buyer.

Richard's notes: It's a cave. Literally a cave. And I don't know what she wants, but to be honest I'll stay in any godforsaken hole that pleases her as long as she can be happy with me and our child. She's grown so much bigger over the past few months, and the baby will be here before we know it. Even she must see that modern people don't raise babies in caves. A fucking cave! She can't possibly want this.

Carolyn's notes: This is better than the others. Fewer distractions. There are horses in the field nearby, which I like. One of my chapters is about Icelanders' conversion to Christianity in the year 1000. They had to follow the religion, obviously, but they were allowed three exceptions. One was the eating of horsemeat – luckily for those horses, we're not Icelandic. The other exceptions were ritual scarification carried out in secret, and *bera út*, abandoning a child in nature to die of exposure. I've tried to tell Richard so many times but he doesn't think it's interesting. Anyway, I don't think this is the right house for us.

The Bird House

Spacious and airy, complete with open skylight. Fantastic views. Comes as seen, trunk and all attached branches included, as well as any feathers. Birds may return to lay eggs, meaning an environmentally friendly and organic food source for owners.

Richard's notes: This is getting ridiculous. We're eight months in and she's enormous, almost past walking. How is she supposed to get up and down a tree? It would be impossible to attach any sort of decent ladder to the trunk, it's so spindly. And that's not even mentioning a child who'll be crawling in no time – right off the branch, no doubt, and what then? And what are we supposed to do when it rains? I need to put my foot down. At least, I would if it wouldn't snap the branch we're standing on.

Carolyn's notes: This is closer. This is better. I need light and air and space and solitude. I need to be able to move, to think. It's not just for me, it's not selfishness. We won't get any more of my advance money until I finish the book. I have to support us all, and I can't do that in the gloom and the earth and the fetid heat. This is nice – open, airy. The twigs are a bit scratchy but there are plenty of feathers and they're very soft. Of course they're soft; that's what people stuff duvets and cushions with. The baby will soon need a home that isn't me, and here's a literal feather bed. We haven't quite found the right place yet, but we're near.

The Island House

This cosy and charming wooden structure is set on its own island. Structure in fact covers the whole island, which is compact and ideally situated in a peaceful and secluded part of the ocean. Ideal for the homeowner who likes their own space.

Richard's notes: Look, I'll admit that it sounded good when the estate agent said we could live on our own island. But when I imagined island life, I did imagine that I'd be able to actually walk on the island. You know what I'm picturing: a beach, some trees, maybe some green patches for chickens or sheep. This one is so tiny that you can't leave the house without stepping into the ocean.

It's not even a calm, blue, tropical sort of ocean – it's grey and choppy and every other wave crashes into the outer walls. I can't believe this is what she wants. The baby is only a few weeks old, and as we're looking around the house I swear she's eyeing up places she could put him down.

Carolyn's notes: What was my life before? What was it like to arrange my time the way I chose? What was it like to be able to hear my own breathing? Three weeks, and I can barely remember. It needs so much. It wants so much. I thought if I could go away, away, away – to an island, no one else there – then I could work. But there will never again be a place with no one else there. I could be on the other side of the world and I would still hear him cry for me in the night. His tiny mouth, never full, never silent.

The Glacier House

A spacious, secluded, one-of-a-kind property created from a much-sought-after glacier. Fully open-plan with far-reaching views to all sides: front, back, top, and bottom (when over deep water). Currently three bedrooms, though further rooms can be carved out.

Richard's notes: Why on earth would she even consider this? Dragging us up to the hinterlands, so far fucking north I feel like we're about to tip off the map. I get that her book is on northern cultures, but come on! She wants to go from a northern country, to a further northern country, and then when she's in that country she wants to go even further? I mean, Christ, why don't we just move to the middle of the Arctic and call it quits? Not only is this house on the ice; it's made of ice, with beds and sofas and tables and chairs made of ice. There are no walls. There is no roof. I can't believe she'd even suggest bringing our child here. The wee guy will freeze to death in about three seconds. *I'm* freezing to death in about three seconds, and I'm a bloody adult, with enough body fat to shame a seal. I can't live here. He can't live here. God, I miss the mushrooms.

Carolyn's notes: The first step I took into this house, I felt my mind flash clear. It's perfection. I can work here, I know it. I love this glacier: the chill, the cleanse of it. We're taking this house. It's everything I need. I think of the horses, of the ritual scarring, of the cold. There are rules to the world, I know. But perhaps there can be exceptions. I don't need three, only one. We'll take it. Are you listening? I'll take it.

I'm just back from the pool, and I've been thinking. As I swim I count laps, and on the lonely walk home I count steps. It's good thinking time. In writing this book, I'm trying to figure things out. I know I'm taking a while to get to any answers, but bear with me. I'm writing my way through.

I want to know what haunts me. The ghosts that obscure my face in the mirror, that speak in my head when I'm trying to think, that pull my hands back when I try to reach out. I know there's something; I just don't know what it is yet.

But also.

This work I'm doing, this dragging up of my worst fears. I don't know what it's doing to me. Maybe I'm looking for something – for someone – to keep me safe. To say that I'm safe, even if it's not true.

We tell ourselves stories, we stoke our fears, we keep them burning. For what? What do we expect to find there inside?

What are we all doing to ourselves?

Half Sick of Shadows

Excalibur

Camelot appears to them through a sudden drop in the trees. The black tips on the white towers. The rusting swoop of the roller coaster. The flap of a tattered flag. In the back seat, the little one clutches her rag doll tight with excitement, making its yellow wool ringlets jerk. The big one in the driver's seat stops the car. The other big one in the passenger seat unclips her seat belt. There is one other vehicle in the enormous car park: a camper van, long-abandoned, its white sides mossed and rusty.

They release the child locks. The little one clambers out of the car, leaving the two big ones in the front seat to talk. There's plenty to hold her attention, as the car park is littered with toys: plastic soldiers, stuffed teddies, configurations of still-bright Lego blocks, a congregation of dolls. She forgets her own doll on the seat. The big ones have to speak quietly; the little one has left her door wide open, as if knowing to leave an escape route.

The Sorcerer

- It's not so bad here, is it? It's actually kind of nice.
  - If you squint. Or close your eyes entirely.

- It'll be fine inside. There are cosy places to rest, things to eat, plenty of other kids. It's like a holiday for her. Kids love adventuring, self-sufficiency, making forts, all that Enid Blyton shit.
- I'm not sure about this. Are we doing the right thing? Maybe if we just…
- Come on, Scarlet, we agreed. You won't care about this tomorrow.

Towers of Fun

The afternoon is already old. Dusty golden light stretches low across the car park, shadowing the stones. The little one patters back over to the car, her buckle shoes gleaming against the cracked asphalt. She holds a doll in one hand, snatched from the silent choir, its hair dirty but still prettily blonde underneath, its cheeks pink circles the size of thumbprints.

She stands patiently at the driver's side window until the two big ones notice her and abruptly stop their muttering. Their smiles stretch wide and painful and they make a performance of getting out of the car and locking the doors, for all the world as if they're getting ready for a lovely day out, for all the world as if the theme park hasn't been abandoned and forgotten for the past ten years.

They walk under the portcullis, arms swinging joyfully, the little one between them. The little one hesitates, hiding the doll behind her back. One of the big ones attempts to whistle a tune, but the notes quickly die. Without meaning to, they all tip back their heads as they pass the white towers of the castle, staring at the empty eyes of the windows.

Dragon Flyer

- What have you got there, my little lily?
- A dolly, Daddy. Can I keep it?

- Where did you get it?
- On the ground when I got out of the car. There are lots of them.
- Are you sure? You're not telling a fib?
- No, Daddy! I promise. It was just left there and nobody dropped it because nobody was there around, not for ages I think. Someone must have not wanted it any more.
- Where's your dolly?
- I forgotted it in the car. I could get it when I get back though, couldn't I, Daddy? Then I don't need this one.
- That's okay, my willow. You keep that one.

Knightmare

Together, the three walk through the theme park, keeping to the ruptured paths where they can. The roller coaster looms and swoops above their heads, and the little one squawks to see it. She doesn't ask to go on it; it's unclear whether she knows that the carts have been rusted in place for years, or whether her own imagination is enough to take her on the ride.

The sky is empty of gold now, slipping into dusty blue. The big ones let the little one stay there under the roller coaster, head tilted up, watching the very beginning of the moon appear in a loop of track.

One of the big ones veers off towards a shadowy building and observes it, thinking. Pale, rain-damaged figures cluster around the lurid signage. Broken multicoloured bulbs flash in the last of the light. The other big one observes the little one for a moment; she goes to take her tiny hand, then thinks better of it. Instead she joins the other big one by the shadowy building.

Dungeons of Doom

- Is this a ghost train?
  - I mean, that's what I'd choose, if it was me. It's inside, it's warm, it's low-lit. Cosy. What do you think?
  - Don, are you seriously fucking telling me that you think a ghost train is a good idea? A clattery cart and tissue-paper ghosts and spooky noises, forever. That's what you want for her? I despair, I really do.
  - You know what? If you've got all the fucking answers then you can just do it yourself. Let me remind you that this was your idea, Scarlet.
  - It might have been my idea, but I didn't want to actually go through with it. We could still change our minds. We could…
  - We couldn't. It's practically done. And we won't know about it by tomorrow. By tonight, even. By the time the stars come out, okay? We'll go back under the portcullis and it will all be over. I promise.

Jousting Knights Dodgems

They walk on. The little one is tiring now, her dolly dragging in the dirt. They pass the caterpillar ride, the galleon, the jousting arena. The big ones are tiring too, getting emotional, neither wanting to voice their doubts in case the other doesn't argue them down. The day is fading and they can hardly see their steps.

A moment of panic: the little one has gone.

They call for her and find her on the dodgems, curled up in a cart.

Pendragon's Plunge

- I don't want to walk any more, Daddy. Are we nearly there?
  - Yes, my shadow. Will I carry you?

- On your shoulders.
- Last time, okay? You're too big for this.
- I'm heavy now, aren't I?
- Yes, my silent night, my bunch of stars, my curse. You are the heaviest.

The Gauntlet

They've looped round the entire empty park – the shattered paths, the dry waterslide, the armless eyeless gormless statues, the silent carousel, the broken chairs, the torn flags, the leaf-choked carts empty and waiting. They're almost back at the car park now. The little one is almost asleep; the big one's hands rest on her white buckle shoes, keeping them tight to his chest so she doesn't tip off his shoulders.

Before them, the portcullis is all in shadow. Beyond it, the moon glints off the car's windscreen. The white turrets with their black tips gleam fairytale-pretty. The big ones avoid each other's eyes. Up the stairs, each step careful. The little one's head nods asleep.

In the top turret, he slides her off his shoulders and lays her gently on the ground. He takes off his coat and lays it over her like a blanket. He backs away.

Don and Scarlet leave their daughter alone in the empty tower and go back to their car.

Human Cannonball

- Don, can't we ... shouldn't we ...
  - She'll be fine. We chose the best place.
  - Was she really that bad? Maybe if we'd tried harder with her. Everyone else manages it.

- We're not everyone else. If everyone else jumped off a bridge, would you?
- I wish I'd never thought of this.
- We're nearly at the portcullis. Soon you'll never think of it again.

Kingdom in the Clouds

They unlock the car and climb in. They're happy; a day at the theme park would cheer anyone up. They can still feel that leaping, bubbly, post-roller-coaster feeling in their throats. They kiss, and break away with a laugh. What a wonderful day it's been.

Don starts the car, then wriggles in his seat. Something is digging into his back. He reaches behind him and pulls out a rag doll. It has yellow wool for hair and a patchwork dress. He sits for a long time staring at it, genuinely confused. Why on earth do they have a rag doll in their car? He holds it up for Scarlet to see, but she only laughs, thinking Don has brought it for some reason, some little in-joke gift for her. Well, never mind. He rolls down the window and throws the doll out. There seem to be a lot of other toys in the car park, for some reason. People are such litterbugs. He turns up the radio and together they drive away, unencumbered, free as a flag in the breeze.

A tragedy can become a horror if you're not allowed to deal with it as a tragedy. Imagine you were having an affair with a married work colleague, and that colleague suddenly died. You would only be allowed to mourn that person distantly, appropriate to a work colleague, not as a lover. Or imagine you were the married one, and you were planning to leave, and then your spouse died and you had to mourn them as if you had loved them still. Or imagine you had a miscarriage early on, and couldn't tell anyone that your child had died, because you hadn't told anyone there was a child in the first place.

Such secrets you would need to swallow. Such masks you would need to wear.

The Only Thing I Can't Tell You is Why

There's a moment, before anyone knows that Thomasin has woken from the anaesthetic, when everything is perfect. The slats of sunlight on the wall. The waltz of silver motes. The promise of her baby, new, born.

She thinks about the birth and how it was agony, but also awful, in the old sense of the word: awe-ful, making her full of awe. She looked behind the green hanging sheet and saw her own blood, an outflow, so much it was black. Death tapped at her window and she turned from it and made life instead. She is happy, and that happiness opens her eyes.

The nurses notice her, two or three of them she thinks, but they blend and merge, don't they, so bright and clean with their quick hands. The nurses bustle into action and wheel a plastic cot over to her. Transparent plastic, with an unrealistically white knitted blanket. She'd never managed to wash anything so white. Thomasin looks inside, and she is excited to see what she has made from nothing, a brand-new life without even having to give up her own, and she presses down the sides of the blanket to see, and there is her baby, and her baby is dead.

It's a boy! Well done you. Look at his tiny hands, he's a wee darling. Shall we try a feed?

Thomasin lifts her baby from the cot, and as she twists she feels her stitches tug, and her baby is dead. She lays her baby on her breast, and lets the nurse help with the latching on, and her baby is dead. She watches her baby grasp and kick, the pucker of the mouth, and she feels the sharp pull of her milk beginning to flow, and her baby is dead. She lies in the hospital bed. The nurses potter around. There is sunlight on the wall. Her baby is dead.

The nurses make her take it home. She calls it Phillip, though it's hard to think of it as anything other than *it*. It – Phillip – coos and blinks in its Ikea cot, kicks its feet in its little fox-print socks, opens its mouth and screams for her. Thomasin lifts her breast to the gasping mouth. If the nurses say it's a baby then she supposes it must be.

The nurses warned her about the baby blues. She repeats the phrases for the feelings she's been told to expect, lets them sit in her mouth: *a persistent sadness, an unspecified anxiety.*

She thinks the phrase 'baby blues' as she looks at its eyes, blue as blueberries, as bluebells, as blue jeans. Its eyes roll back in its head as it feeds, ecstatic as a saint. Thomasin looks at the wall until it's finished.

Two weeks later, the paternity leave is up and her husband goes back to work. Her baby is dead. When it makes a noise like crying, she feeds it or changes its nappy or burps it or carries it around stroking its sturdy, bendable back that vibrates with each cry and wondering how many decibels of her hearing she's losing from its screaming right against her ear. With her free hand she thumb-taps on her phone: *how loud is baby cry*. A baby's cry can be about 130 decibels, which is louder than a thunderclap or a chainsaw or a Boeing 737 aircraft at one nautical mile (6076ft) before landing. The internet assures her that a baby's cry cannot rupture anyone's eardrums.

All her clothes reek of old milk. Under her fingernails she can smell vomit no matter how many times she scrubs them. She doesn't find jokes funny but does find a shrieking laugh bubbling up her throat at inappropriate times.

She walks around the house in circles. She does not think a responsible mother would put in earplugs to lessen the decibels of a screaming baby, even if it protects her hearing, so she doesn't. But she wants to.

In the end, it's a good thing that her baby is dead, because she's no mother.

Her husband comes home after work and heats up a bottle of milk that Thomasin expressed earlier. He walks around the house without seeing anything, so focused is he on his task of feeding. His shoulders and shins bump into walls and tables and he doesn't seem to feel it. He coos to it – to Phillip – as he walks.

What a baby booboo, dada loves you, can you say gaga for me, say dada? You booboo looloo love to you-you.

If her husband says it's a baby then she supposes it must be. For dinner they have spaghetti hoops on toast and a glass of milk; little-kid food. Her head throbs too much to cook and her husband says it's a treat. Later in bed they turn away from the cot and have sex. Her baby is dead.

*

One day Thomasin goes to the park with Phillip and her mother, because if her mother says it's a baby then she supposes it must be. At first the park feels like a revelation. Black wings lift from in front of her eyes, the black cloud dissipates. She even feels like she might want to wash her hair when she gets home.

Because she realises that her baby is not the only one. There, swinging on the swings and sliding down the slide, are other dead children. Not all of them are dead, but some. They're easy to identify.

She sidles up to a mother of one of these children and, without thinking about what she's going to say, all in a rush she asks how she should be a mother to a dead baby. The other mother smiles politely and takes a clear step away from Thomasin before she speaks.

You must be mistaken. My child is right there. Look, can you see? On the see-saw. She has curly hair and pink overalls. She loves the see-saw.

Thomasin tries again, desperate for solidarity. But the other mother walks away and scoops up her pink-overalled child, who Thomasin can clearly see is dead, and despite the little girl's protests the other mother takes her to the other side of the park and gets her an ice cream and shows her how to play hopscotch.

Thomasin watches all of this. Then after the other mother has left, Thomasin suggests to her mother that they scoop up Phillip and take him to the other side of the park and get him an ice cream and show him how to play hopscotch. Her mother is so pleased that she cries, then smiles through the tears, which somehow makes it worse.

Thomasin doesn't know what to do. So she does what everyone tells her to do, what the other mothers do, what it says to do in the books even when the books contradict one another. She does it all right, everything she can.

Phillip grows bigger, and he starts school, and he finishes school, and he starts university, and he finishes university, and he goes and gets a job and a wife and a house, and Thomasin is there for all of it, wearing her best clothes, her blow-dried hair, her string of pearls, there in the front row and at the top table, there so proud, clapping and happy-crying, experiencing the most joyful moment of her life after the moment she lay in the hospital after the birth looking at the sun on the wall waiting to meet her baby, and through all the years of it she knows, knows without a moment of doubt, that her child is dead.

I lied to you. I'm sorry.

There is no baby.

There was, and now there isn't.

It's nice to think that if you try hard, you'll be rewarded. It's nice to think that if you name a fear, it can't come true. It's nice to think that even if it does come true, it can't possibly be as bad as you think.

But there it is: I feared that we wouldn't get to have this baby, and my fear came true, and it was even worse than I imagined.

PART 3:
THE PAST

'It is so dark inside the wolf.'
– The Brothers Grimm

I lied to you about the house and the wife too. I'm sorry.

There's no one at home waiting for me. There's no home.

I had a house and a wife, and then I didn't.

I shouldn't have lied to you, I know that. It's just – I'm scared, and it hurts, and I wanted to pretend that things were different. I won't lie to you again.

That's what liars always say, isn't it? That every lie is the last.

But this time. I promise.

One thing I know I can be truthful about is my past. The older I get and the more I lose, the more I cling to this. I want to wander through the lush gardens of my childhood, to get calmly and sweetly and woozily lost in the maze of memory.

There are things there I have forgotten, and I want to rediscover them. Even when everything else is lost, there's still somewhere to find comfort.

I should tell you: I'm still in Iceland. I know it's been a while, but there doesn't seem to be any harm in me staying a little longer. I'm in my writing studio. It's at a distance from the cabin where I sleep, and the walls are lined with windows. I've been writing all day, and I forgot to put the lights on. I've just noticed how dark it is here.

I should get up. I should put the lights on. But it's so nice here in the dark.

I'll Eat You Up
I Love You So

First Fear:

The Callipaed advised Evangeline to avoid looking at bears, lest she have a hairy child; dogs, lest she have a vicious child; and elephants, lest she have a lumpy and misshapen child (this, said the book, was the mistake made by the elephant man Joseph Merrick's mother). Ideally, Evangeline shouldn't just avoid these animals in life: she should avoid looking at pictures of all undesirable creatures, or even thinking of them. The link between mother and baby was that strong. This once-popular theory of maternal impression was now considered outdated, worthy only of ridicule. But getting pregnant had cost Evangeline a lot of money and effort, and at her age I was her last chance. Desperate people will risk anything. Even ridicule.

Evangeline replaced all the pictures in the house – family photos, dull landscapes, bizarre paintings by her old art school friends – with images of insects on vellum. Insects, thought Evangeline, have the power to transform. Larvae to beetles, maggots to flies, caterpillars to butterflies. This was something that Evangeline wanted for me.

She lay back on her clean sheets, eating fingers of mango from a bowl, and stared hard at her new pictures. She tried to push the images through her brain, down her body, along the umbilical cord and to me. But then she looked at the mango. Did she really want me to have the properties of a mango? Easily bruised and susceptible to powdery mildew? She went into the garden and threw the fruit on the grass. Then she sat very still on the back step until insects started to convene. She let them eat a bit, just to be nice, then she scooped the insects into her bowl and took them inside. Using a cocktail stick, she speared each insect and put it in her mouth. She thought hard about them as she swallowed them; of the insects' transformations that she wished to absorb and pass on to me.

It wasn't enough. She only had one chance to get it right. So she took the insects into her home, her bed, her body. And when I finally came, after all those months of Evangeline eating only insects and sleeping on a bed of insects and speaking only to insects and looking only at insects and allowing insects to crawl on and in her – well, I was exactly as you would expect.

The other children at school did not like me. They followed me to the toilets and hung over the cubicle, pointing and laughing. They spat on me outside the school gates. They pretended they couldn't hear or understand me when I spoke, until I began to wonder whether I was actually speaking only in my head, or perhaps accidentally in a foreign language. They stole from me and kicked at me and if I had been tiny like a bug they would have squashed me under their shoes.

One day they followed me home from school and waited until I was at the empty fields at the edge of town, and among the red dust and sun-faded litter they beat me up quite a lot. When they'd left, I lay there, bleeding into the earth. I'd been there what felt like a long time, but was actually only just past teatime, when the insects emerged.

At home, Evangeline waited. She knew something terrible had happened to me. I'd told her about the mean boys at school, and she'd had some serious talks with their mothers and the teachers. It had only made things worse. Boys do not like to be told what to do.

But she didn't worry about me, not yet. She knew, deep down, that I was already being helped. She could picture it all so clearly: the ants would staple up my wounds with their sharp heads, even though they got decapitated in the process. The earwigs would lie protectively over my bloody parts until they clotted, even though some of the earwigs drowned in the blood. The bees would come next, dropping sweet nectar into my mouth. Insects that usually ate other insects would feed me too, once the nectar had honeyed my throat so they could slip right down. I was one of them – she had made sure of that – so she knew they would help me.

When dusk came, the moths would take their turn, lying down with their soft wings spread, hundreds of them covering my body entirely. Her little boy would never have known a blanket so soft and living. I would dream of all the insects banding together and chasing after the bad boys who hurt me and making them hurt back. Lots of the moths would be crushed when I rolled over in my sleep, and lots more would freeze in the cold night to keep me warm. It was a nice picture for my mother, wasn't it? Hundreds of insects sacrificing themselves to save one solitary boy.

But.

Evangeline had consumed a lot of insects while I was inside her, and that meant I had consumed a lot too. Insects may have short lives individually, but together they have long memories.

In the soft pink dawn, just as Evangeline was starting to fear that she had made a terrible mistake, the insects came down from the trees and up from the soil and over from the bushes and convened on me. Piece by piece they pulled me apart, and took me home to feed to their babies, and they never once worried about the outdated theory of maternal impression.

Second Fear:

The worst thing about going to other people's houses was not that it smelled weird, or that the chairs were too hard so your bones hurt or too soft so they swallowed you, or that they had a guinea pig that squeaked or a baby sister that dribbled, or that they watched different things on TV, or that you had to ask to go to the toilet. It was the food.

Why did the orange juice have bits in it? Why did the bread have seeds in it? Why was the cereal the wrong brand? Why did they drink so much tea? Why did the soup have to be mushroom?

Clarice had asked herself these questions often, because every day after school she had to go to her neighbour Mrs Dainty's house. Mrs Dainty had been trying to teach Clarice how to use the right cutlery and play the piano and say *pardon* and *yes, miss* for a while now, and it wasn't going very well.

This pattern repeated for a few months when one Monday, after Mrs Dainty had failed to teach Clarice a thing and Clarice had failed to learn it, she went out of the room and came back in with a miniature apple on a plate.

'It's a gold and delicious apple,' said Mrs Dainty. 'Eat it all up now.'

It was indeed gold, bright shiny gold, even the stalk and the tiny leaf attached to it. Clarice lifted the apple from the plate and brought it to her mouth. It was the size of a golf ball and it smelled waxy, like a candle, and also painty. She scratched at the gold and it scraped off and collected under her fingernail, revealing its dense yellowy innards. She did not want it in her mouth.

Luckily, Mrs Dainty then went out of the room again, probably to make yet more tea, so Clarice opened the window and threw the apple into the garden. It rolled under a shrub; Clarice wanted to go outside and kick it further to hide it, but she didn't. She closed the window silently and crept back to her chair. Mrs Dainty shuffled back in with chinking tea things on a tea tray and looked at Clarice's empty plate.

'You ate it all? The inside too?'

'Was I not meant to?' asked Clarice. Mrs Dainty frowned so she added – 'Miss?' Mrs Dainty still didn't say anything, so she added – 'Thank you, miss, it was lovely,' and that seemed to do the trick.

It all happened again on Tuesday: the gold and delicious, the window, the throwing.

But on Wednesday, Mrs Dainty did not go out of the room. Clarice thought about asking for some tea, but you could never ask Mrs Dainty for things unless you wanted to hear for a long time about what an ungrateful child you were. There was nothing else for it. Clarice put the apple in her mouth.

It tasted very gold, and not delicious. At first Clarice tried to bite it, but the spongy give of it made her stomach clench. Instead she pushed it far back in her mouth and swallowed it whole. By the time the apple had gone down, her eyes were watering.

Of course Mrs Dainty would not have given her neighbour's child a wax apple covered in spray-paint to eat. But it certainly tasted like it.

Mrs Dainty smiled to see Clarice swallowing the apple. The next day, when she brought another small golden apple and Clarice swallowed it, Mrs Dainty smiled again. Actually, with each passing day she smiled a lot more in general. She didn't tell Clarice that she was an ungrateful child, and brought her a gold and delicious apple every afternoon and watched as she swallowed it whole. It wasn't just the smiling. Mrs Dainty seemed looser, somehow; like she was always slow-dancing to a song in her head. She talked more and she ate more and she even laughed occasionally.

After several years, Clarice was old enough to take care of herself after school, and she didn't go to Mrs Dainty's any more. She still could not play the piano, but she usually remembered to say *pardon*, though that was really all she said; the assemblage of apples sat heavy and painful in her stomach, up her gullet and right to the back of her throat, so that she rarely spoke or ate or moved when she didn't have to.

Clarice stopped being a girl and became a woman instead, and eventually an old lady. Her first husband died young and the second one died old, but not as old as Clarice, and after he died she realised she had never really liked him. She didn't want his name any more, so she changed it to Dainty; she'd always liked that name, and now that she was older it suited her. As a child she had been so restless, so noisy, so greedy; she was grateful that she had grown out of it to be a proper lady. She had eventually learned to play the piano, and liked to give lessons to the local children.

One Monday, her neighbour's child came over for a piano lesson. Clarice went into her kitchen to make some tea. The child could be a pretty thing - she had pale hair and lovely tapering fingers. But it was a shame: she was so noisy, and such a fidget. Always shifting in her seat and leaping about and talking about one thing or another, and never calling her *miss*. Clarice cleared her throat delicately. If only the child could learn to be more refined, more respectful, more still. Clarice cleared her throat harder. She'd managed it, hadn't she? All children learned eventually. You mustn't question grown-ups and you must always eat everything on your plate. Clarice cleared her throat; it was almost a cough now, though she was too much of a lady for such sounds.

Clarice Dainty finished making her tea and got a small plate out of the cupboard. She reached deep into her throat, and she pulled out the malformed pieces of wax that had been lodged there for almost her entire life, and she formed the wax into the shape of an apple, and she painted it gold, and she put it on a plate. She carried the tray through and put the plate down in front of the child.

'It's a gold and delicious apple,' said Mrs Dainty. 'Eat it all up now.'

Third Fear:

Veronica spent most of her troublesome pregnancy resting on a chaise longue. It was upholstered in pink velvet, the colour of a cow's tongue, and it was stuffed with horsehair. Veronica liked it particularly because it's where her child was conceived; she enjoyed reclining like a lady, sighing and sipping weak sugared tea brought by her fussing mother, and remembering how her husband The Doctor had taken her roughly from behind across the cushions, thrusting into her so hard his fingers left dents in the flesh of her hips.

There was a hole in the pink velvet of the chaise longue. Veronica liked to poke her pinkie finger into it. The hole grew a little bigger every day, as did Veronica's belly. Before long a bit of horsehair began to poke out of the hole in the chaise longue. To keep things tidy, Veronica tugged out the stray strands – but what a shame to throw it away; this horsehair was a part of the chaise longue, and the chaise longue was a part of her baby's conception. She put it in her mouth and swallowed it.

By the time Veronica's baby was due, she'd eaten almost all of the horsehair out of the chaise longue. The cushions were just empty fabric over the springs, and as well as a baby inside Veronica, there was also a large hairball.

When they took the baby out of Veronica's body, they took the hairball out too. Veronica named the baby Seth, and the hairball Tawny.

Seth and Tawny developed well, but to be honest Tawny developed a little better. Seth always smelled of poo or sick or old milk, and Veronica spent much of his first few years cleaning him. Tawny kept his shape well, and never smelled of anything other than the inside of an old sofa, a smell which Veronica liked as it reminded her of her husband The Doctor.

Eventually Seth noticed that his mother preferred Tawny. All siblings think this, particularly elder ones, but in this case it was true. Tawny managed to be mouldable, shapeable; but at the same time sturdy and permanent, like the absolute best furniture you can get. But Seth had a body that would not stop leaking and consuming. It farted and burped and snotted and scabbed and earwaxed. It sweated. It made smells. It got dirty and oily. Seth tried to be neat, but his body betrayed him.

One night he crept to the bed where Tawny lay sleeping and pulled a single strand of horsehair from his shoulder. He just wanted to see what it felt like. The strand was wiry and strong, and it smelled like his mother. Seth pulled out a few more strands and wrapped them tight to make a plug, which he inserted into his ear. It did a good job at stopping the earwax getting out, and if Seth couldn't hear in that ear – well, Veronica didn't speak to him that much anyway.

The next night, Seth crept again to Tawny's bed and pulled a few strands of horsehair out. Then a few more. There were so many leaky parts of Seth that needed to be stopped.

Tawny got smaller. And then smaller again. Veronica despaired. She didn't even notice that Seth was much improved; not quite a perfect child, but better than before. With all his orifices blocked, he was significantly less leaky, and therefore less smelly and dirty.

Veronica did everything she could to save Tawny, but it did not occur to her that Seth could be behind it all. Although smaller, Tawny was still perfect. Actually, Tawny was even more perfect than before.

Tawny was cute, even cuter than a sewn poppet, and could be dressed in the most darling dolls' clothes. Tawny could be picked up and carried in a skirt pocket. Tawny could be carried from place to place and displayed delightfully to friends and strangers alike. Tawny never grew oily or crusted. Seth's bulky filthiness grew ever more apparent the bigger he got.

Finally, one day when Veronica was leaning over the stove making a thimble of hot milk for Tawny, Seth reached into her skirt pocket and snatched Tawny out and threw him onto the fire.

Veronica heard a squeal but thought it was just the milk reaching its boiling point.

After that, there was no more horsehair to stop up Seth, and there was no more Tawny to prefer. Veronica loved her leaky, smelly, only child, and every night warmed a cup of milk for him and cuddled him on her lap and read him stories.

Seth, unfortunately, did not enjoy the constant observation and his mother's cloying, needy, wheedling attention. He missed Tawny. But there was nothing to be done about that.

Fourth Fear:

Oh, you. You have always been so delicious. Since the days of your babyhood, when you lay on the rug fresh-washed and kicking the air, grown-ups couldn't help but squeal and bring you to their mouths and kiss you and kiss you and kiss you.

Your tiny toes like cocktail sausages. Your legs fat and juicy as a roasted chicken. Your sweet little belly button dusted with sugary baby powder. Your cheeks icing-pink, your eyes chocolate-brown, your mouth a cherry pout. You're a whole meal from toe to top.

As you get older you won't grow less delicious. Just differently delicious. A sugar-sticky child to a ripe-fruit teenager to an elegant platter of a woman. You will paint and arrange and scent every part of your body so neatly, a cordon bleu chef serving up yourself. You can't blame them for wanting you, can you? It's just a little taste. Just a nibble, no harm done. A single mouthful savoured and swallowed.

But you're not there yet. Still so little and edible. Toddling on your pork-chop legs, grasping things in your fat salty fists. All the aunties and uncles arrive in a mass and swoop you up, cooing and squealing, you're so gorgeous, so perfect, can you imagine ever being so little and perfect? Oh! They could just Eat! You! Up!

They said they would. Although you couldn't talk back, you understood what they said. And you knew it was just a joke, a strange grown-up joke, the way grown-ups always did strange things.

But they did say. You were fair warned. You may kick your little meat-legs and you may weep your seasoning tears and you may cry for them to put you down, but it's too late now.

Their mouths are so big and they open them so wide and inside their teeth are so sharp – and they love you, they love you, they love you so.

I stopped in at the shop today to get some supplies: ground coffee, a big tub of skyr, cubed horsemeat. The meat is tough and has to be cooked for hours, but that doesn't matter. I have time.

As I handed over my money, the overhead fluorescents flickered out. The cashier rolled her eyes and used the torch on her phone to light the buttons on her till. I asked her if that happened often; if there was a problem with the electricity here, lightning storms maybe, faulty wiring. But she didn't reply. I was embarrassed, thinking my accent was too thick and she couldn't understand my English, so I just smiled and took my change and left.

When I was almost back at the cabin I cleared my throat, which was raspy and furred through lack of use. I realised then that the cashier hadn't replied because I hadn't spoken the words aloud at all; I'd said them only in my head.

The World's More Full of Weeping Than You Can Understand

Dorothy's mother took her out for a nice time on the seaside pier one Saturday. There was a lady[1] in a green wool dress[2] showing pictures in a nice book[3], and a

---

1 The lady had a smile that was so white and so wide that it couldn't have been real, and it wasn't; it was a large china shard that she held between her lips and that stretched her mouth into a crescent moon, her cheeks squished into pink balls and her lips pulled out until the skin cracked.

2 The dress was nipped tight at the waist and had a big full skirt, so big that when she sat it touched the ground and made a tent shape. She read stories and her voice was pretty and a bit lisping, and it made little boys want to crawl under her skirt to play, and they did, and they were never seen again.

3 The book had lots of diagrams and guides and it showed how you could make rainy-day projects like a tie-down holder so someone could be hung, drawn and quartered (you needed horses for this so it wasn't very practical), an iron

clown[4], and a Punch[5] and Judy[6] show, and a little penny peepshow machine[7].

---

maiden (you needed an adult for that one, to help with the soldering) or a scold's bridle (only boys were allowed to make that one, though girls could wear it after).

4 Stubble and volcanic sore-looking acne protruded through the clown's face paint, making his skin bumpy like papier mâché. His suit must have been white once, but the armpits and crotch were yellowed with sweat. He spent a long time licking his lips before blowing up his balloons, filling the rubber with his rank breath. When he twisted the balloons they squealed as if in pain, their shapes too bulbous and misshapen to be recognisable as animals.

5 Mister Punch had a white hat, but the more he beat Judy and the red flew out of her eyes the more the white was covered until there was none left at all and his hat was red and his jacket was red and his face was red and when he smiled wide even his teeth were red. It was not a good idea to sit in the front row because then you'd get red too.

6 At first Judy tried to get away from Mister Punch but it was pointless; he was bigger than her and he had a stick, and the more he hit her with it the more bent and broken her limbs became and so eventually she couldn't even crawl away and had to just lie there and blink and breathe until she couldn't do either any more. And then it was the end of the show and everybody clapped.

7 The eyepieces were thick black rubber that looked wet but wasn't, and when you pulled your face away from them the suction felt too strong like it could pull out your eyes if it wanted. When you put your penny in the peepshow was triggered: a trap snapped on a tiny mouse and broke its back, caught it squeaking and squealing and dripping red from its eyes until it died; a guillotine snipped down on the neck of a little brown bird; loops of barbed wire suddenly tightened on a spider, its legs tangling round its fat oozing body. It must all have been made of horsehair and woodchip but it all looked so real.

Last of all, in a dark tent right at the end of the pier, was the magic show. There were rabbits[8] and birds[9] in the magic show.

Then the rabbits and birds went away and there was a lady in a sparkly outfit and a man[10] in a black cape and a box[11] that the lady went inside. She was smiling[12].

Dorothy didn't like it when the lady went into the box but her mother told her to sit still and not worry.

---

8 The rabbits had pink eyes and pink gums and pink inside their noses, and when they got pulled out of the hats only parts of them came out, it was like they split halfway and half got left inside the hat.

9 The birds were very small and their bones seemed very light and when the box collapsed on them the blood all stayed inside like they were never there in the first place.

10 The man was dressed all in black to hide the stains and he unrolled a black leather wrap like a chef's and it was full of knives with black handles and gleaming silver blades; they clicked together and when he chose one he slid it from its black leather loop and very, very gently touched it to his moustache to show how sharp it was, making a single black hair spiral off and see-saw to the floor.

11 The box had writing on it, something with a lot of exclamation marks, but it was too hard to read the words because of all the scratches and scrapes, a long time of blades against the paint.

12 That smile was made of china too, almost definitely china, because if you listened carefully it squeaked and scraped as the woman tried to open her splitting mouth wider to spit it out.

When the lady was in the box the man stuck some shiny knives in[13]. Then he sawed[14] the box in half and separated the two halves[15]. In one side the lady's head was smiling wide. In the other side her toes wiggled[16].

Dorothy didn't understand how the lady could do that but her mother told her to sit still because it was only a trick, not real[17]. Dorothy thought the man was going to put the lady back together, after. But he didn't.

---

13 They made a noise going in, the knives, a pork-chop-chopping type of noise, and the woman shuddered in her box and her smile squeaked and almost broke, and though her eyes rolled back they were still open. Finally all that was visible of the knives was their handles, and they gleamed black and shiny in the lights.

14 The saw was big and rusted and when the man unveiled it he played a wibbly-wobbly dirge on it, and everyone liked that and laughed and didn't notice the woman wasn't wiggling her toes any more.

15 He tilted the boxes away from everyone watching so you couldn't see inside, and it was either because what was inside was so good that he wanted to be the only one to enjoy it, or because it was so terrible that he didn't want everyone else to suffer.

16 They didn't really. It was just the man shaking the box; you could see it if you really looked.

17 But it was real. You knew it was true no matter what anyone said. It was the realest real thing and the woman was really hurt and she was really dying and your mother sat in her seat and smiled too wide with her hand in a vice around your wrist and told you to be good and safe and nice and sit still and don't look at the man, just keep your eyes down and your smile wide, and so you couldn't move to help the woman, because no one ever comes to help.

Instead the curtain[18] came down, and the show was over, and Dorothy and her mother went home[19]. It was all a nice trick and they had a nice time.

---

18 The curtain was flesh-coloured and too thick to flutter. In stamped red letters it said FIRE CURTAIN and from its invasive, meaty smell you knew that it had held back many fires.

19 And you went home, you went home, and there was a man in black already there, and through everything that happened to you and your mother, you both had to smile, smile, smile.

The pool is quieter every time I go. Other than the guy on reception, I'm often the only person there. Sometimes there are signs that someone was around recently: a snarl of long blonde hair by the side of the hot tub, an abandoned hairpin on the changing-room floor.

I collect up the things and put them on the same bench, just to see if they're still there when I come back.

I do my laps. A hundred of them. I count each one. I swim until the sky blues out to black and the stars start to appear. Then I do my steps back to my cabin. I count them too. Sometimes I count out loud, just to hear a voice.

There used to be more people around me. I'm sure there were. I saw them. I spoke to them. Not in Icelandic, and not in any depth, but still. I'm sure I spoke.

I got myself into a bit of a daze while I was swimming today – 'story brain', I call it; that hazy, unreal, half-dreaming place where I go to find stories. I go into it after a long time of repetitive movement like swimming or walking, or after listening to wordless music, or on long car journeys. I went into my daze, and through it all I counted my laps, and then walking home I counted my steps.

All the way home I was still there, in story brain, conscious of enough to keep my feet on the path instead of the road, but not much else. It wouldn't have mattered if I had walked in the road, really, as I didn't see a single car. No lights were on in any of the houses. I'd been the only person in the pool. Not even anyone at reception; I'd left my little entry ticket on the counter. Changed, swam, showered, all alone. But the building was open, so someone must have been around.

There must be someone here, somewhere, even if I can't see them.

Sleep Long, Sleep Tight, it is Best to Wake Up Late

You have the right to refuse to fill out this questionnaire, to stop at any time, and to skip over any part of the questionnaire that disturbs you too much. We do advise, however, that you complete the questionnaire as fully as you can, as it is only as good as your level of honesty.

You have the right to anonymity, and your information will be kept confidential. Your information will never be seen individually but only in the aggregate with other responses. Your information will not be sold to strangers or shared on internet message boards.

- How many hours a night do you sleep?
- How would you class your sleep quality?
- Is this:
  - Continuous sleep, i.e. you do not wake no matter what happens to you?
  - Broken sleep, i.e. you wake when things happen to you?

- Describe the last dream you can remember. Please include as much detail as you can.
- Describe your most common recurring dream. Again, please include detail.
- Who told you it was a dream?
- Have you ever woken during the night feeling sure that someone was in your home?
- Were they just inside the front door, waiting downstairs, just past the foot of the bed, or closer?
- At such times do you find yourself paralysed, i.e. unable to move or cry out?
- At such times do you find yourself unwilling to move or cry out even if you could?
- Describe as many of the features of this experience as you can.
- Describe the position in which you were sleeping, what you did just before going to bed, and any other of your behaviours that might be to blame for the experience.
- When the worst incident happened, did you experience any of the following:
  - No physical injuries?
  - Minor physical injuries (bruises and cuts that did not require stitches)?
  - Serious physical injuries (stitches, broken nose, broken bones, or hospitalisation)?
- When the best incident happened, did you experience any of the following:
  - No physical injuries?
  - Minor physical injuries (bruises and cuts that did not require stitches)?

- Serious physical injuries (stitches, broken nose, broken bones, or hospitalisation)?
- How much did you like it?
- Do you know any ways of preventing this experience? If so, please give them.
- Why do you never do the things that prevent the experience?
- Why do you like the experience?
- How many would be your preferred number to be hiding inside the home?
- What would you most like them to do to you?
- Were you asleep the last time they came?
- Were you only pretending to be asleep?
- Do you wish for the experience again?
- Are you sure it was a dream?
- Are you sure it was a stranger?

Please leave your completed questionnaire in the appropriate box. You may then go home and wait.

Something happened on the way back from the pool today. By the time I did my laps and walked back to my cabin, it was dark. The black sky, the black road, everything merging. I was in outer space, I was at the bottom of the sea.

And then, far off to my right, in what I thought I remembered was an empty field: a light. At first I thought it was a car driving towards me with only one headlight working. But the light was too low, and it wasn't moving. Half blind in the dark, shuffling so I wouldn't trip on the scrubby grass, I moved off the path and onto the field. As I got closer to the light my brain turned possibilities over, seeing which would fit. A fallen street light. An enormous eye. A sudden floodlight set, for some reason, into the bare earth.

It was a torch. Still lit, dropped to the ground. It's ridiculous, I know, but I didn't dare call out. I couldn't help feeling like it was a trap. I kicked the torch and watched the swoop of light. I picked up the torch and trained it over the field. Nothing but bare ground.

I clicked off the torch and put it back where I found it. I don't know why I did that; I just didn't want to be in my cabin and still be able to see that tiny lighthouse in the middle of nothing.

Exquisite Corpse

She reclines, lascivious, motionless, on velvet and satin cushions. Her back is caught in a slight arch, as if she's pressing her breasts into a hand that reaches for her. Her pink nipples point to the ceiling. Her breasts are full and round. Her waist is tiny, narrow enough for a man's hands to circle.

Her skin is ivory, poreless. Her eyes are tilted half open. Her eyelashes are soft and black and real. Her hair is warm honey, flowing over the cushions, curling to perfection at the tips, all real. On top of it is nestled a pearl tiara.

Her underarms and legs are smooth, her pubic hair small and soft like a pad of moss, neatly trimmed but still thick enough to be a hiding place, and that is real too. She wears nothing, clothed only her own post-orgasmic bliss.

*

When the dwarfs came home that evening they found Snow White lying on the ground.

*

191

That night in her bedroom, Stokeley arranges her pillows carefully then reclines lasciviously. She waits. She tries to be motionless but the brushes and Delilah's breath tickle.

'Don't smile! It makes your eyelids crinkle.'

Stokeley purses her lips hard so her face doesn't move. Delilah smells of cake and cherry and watermelon and coconut and dulce de leche; on the way home from the museum they tested all the body sprays until the pharmacist made them leave.

'Hello and welcome to my make-up tutorial. Follow every step or you are a moron and ugly.'

Through Stokeley's eyelids, the light is pink. Delilah strokes a brush across Stokeley's eyelid and the light dims.

'First I apply a base colour for an even look. I am using a beige but you can use whatever colour suits your model's skin tone.'

Ugh, beige. Why not ivory? Stokeley wills her pores to shrink.

Delilah goes away then comes back with the brush again, which she presses a little too hard on Stokeley's eyelids. The light flashes in orange and purple zigzags. She'd pull back but there's nowhere to go, and Delilah's breath smells like candyfloss.

'Next I apply an accent colour to really make the model's eye colour pop. And I don't mean like Stan in Geography's eyes, which just pop anyway, especially when one of the girls bends over to pick up the big atlas.'

Stokeley purses her lips to hold in her smile and keep her face uncreased.

'Lie still. I have to do the highlight now.'

Delilah has put her favourite playlist on and Stokeley wants to mouth the verses to her, the parts the boy sings before the girl comes in for the chorus. The light is pink and then dark and then pink and then dark. She can feel the heat of Delilah close to her, examining her work. Stokeley doesn't know if she can open her eyes yet. She doesn't want to.

'You're so pretty like that.'

For a second Stokeley thinks Delilah is still doing her fake video narration. She does a stupid duck-face pout and flutters her eyelashes, but through her blinking eyes she sees that Delilah is pulling away from her, lips closing, eyes turning away.

*

Lie still. You're so pretty like that.

*

Stokeley wanted to do Delilah's make-up in return – to be so close her breath would stir Delilah's eyelashes, to see the peachy fuzz along her jaw and top lip; to trace the contours of her, even if only with a brush; to have a good reason to look at her face, and not have the burning scrutiny of her looking back.

But when she reaches for the brushes, Delilah takes them and clicks open the palettes. She turns to the mirror and does her own make-up and it is quick, functional, unnarrated. Stokeley pretends to read a magazine and not watch Delilah. She glances up after every sentence.

'Which quiz do you want? You can have Which Celebrity is Older, What Kind of Flirt Are You, What Should You Dress Up As For Halloween, What's Your Girl Power Anthem, or Does Your Crush Secretly Love You?'

'Last one,' murmurs Delilah to her reflection. She smears on base that's the same colour as her skin but flatter.

'Question one. Your crush shows up unexpectedly, and you're halfway through your beauty routine and not looking the way you'd like. Do you hide away so he doesn't see you in disarray, or see him anyway as he'll still fancy you?'

Delilah opens a shadow palette, the colours pink and yellow and red. She wields brushes. She glares at her own face like she's angry with it.

'Question two. When you tell your crush that you think a rock star is hot, does he agree or sulk or fire back that he fancies a sexy actress?'

Delilah blends in some things along her cheeks that are darker than her skin, then some other things that are lighter. When she has finished she looks unspeakably more beautiful than Stokeley, who now feels like a drag queen in her smoky eye and purple lip, the harsh line of her blush. She feels sick with envy. She won't be that beautiful until she's dead.

'Question three. If you had a problem, would you go to your crush first? Does your crush come to you first? Who reveals the most?'

Delilah finishes with a slick of pink gloss, and Stokeley waits for her to blow an air-kiss – it doesn't even have to be to Stokeley, it can be to Delilah's own reflection. Instead Delilah sits still and examines her own face in the mirror, assessing, judging. She sighs and turns away from it.

Stokeley prepares the words: *you're so beautiful, the most beautiful one, they'd take your hair and put it on the models, I'd take your hair, I'd climb inside you, I'd put your skin on and walk around, let me, let me.* Thankfully the doorbell rings and she pounds downstairs to let in Marybeth and Casey and Zeke before her dad gets to the door.

The downstairs hall smells of shit and she holds her breath and dashes into the bathroom and pushes the window wide open. Please let it all go before they notice it. Please.

*

They were going to bury her, but she still looked as fresh as a living person.

*

The models in the museum are called anatomical Venuses or slashed beauties. But Delilah likes their other name, *dissected graces*, better. It feels more intentional.

'All the hair is real,' says the tour guide. 'Both on the head and, uh, and elsewhere. It was taken from corpses.'

'Oh my actual God,' whispers Delilah into Stokeley's ear. 'Corpse pubes.'

Stokeley snorts a laugh and goes to comment back into Delilah's ear, but she's ducked down to look more closely at the case, leaning right over like she wants to whisper something to the dissected grace and doesn't want anyone else to hear.

'Who did it?' Stokeley says out loud, which is what she meant to say into Delilah's ear.

Everyone, including the tour guide, turns to look at Stokeley.

'Who did what?' asks the tour guide, with the suspicious manner of someone who isn't sure if this is a kid about to do a fart joke.

'The, uh, the hair. Who cut it? Seems like a, uh–' Stokeley is aware her voice is trembling; she talks louder and lighter to fight it, tries to be a cute girl making a cute joke. 'Seems like a funny sort of job to get. Short straw, sort of thing. The head hair, I mean, I'm asking about the head hair, not the … other.'

And now everyone is thinking about corpse pubes, is visualising someone approaching a dead body with a little plastic bag and a comb and a pair of scissors and a creepy look on their face, hungry almost, snick-snacking the scissors with every step, looming like Edward Scissorhands, and because Stokeley brought up the subject of course they're all picturing her doing it.

'Ugh,' mutters Casey, 'grossness,' and she's looking at Stokeley.

And Stokeley can't bear to look back at Casey, so she looks at Delilah, who's still gazing down at the dissected grace – long black hair, body blooming from an open cavity of petal-like organs, the colours of autumn leaves and antique lace.

'Well,' says the tour guide, calm and smoothing, 'I imagine an anatomy student would have dealt with the corpses. That's who these models were for, you see: anatomy students. They were all men in those days. Not like today with our gender equality and everything.'

The tour goes on, the boys snickering, the girls pretending to ignore them.

'You'll notice,' continues the tour guide, 'that the models are all female, so there was a good gender balance in the anatomy rooms. Some people think that the male anatomy students found it easier to confront death in the opposite sex. Or perhaps they just liked to look at pretty girls.'

Don't we all, hangs the obvious reply, like a fart in the air, but no one says it.

*

Who reveals the most?

*

Delilah and Marybeth and Casey and Zeke are all in Stokeley's room, arrayed across her bed, limbs cocked, long hair spread and fluttering.

Stokeley is in the downstairs bathroom, and she can hear them all laughing and singing along to the music. She went in the bathroom to try to make the smell of her dad's shit go out faster, because she doesn't want them to think it's her shit and also because she doesn't want them to think she lives in a house that smells like shit.

She sits on the toilet, not shitting, just because it's the only place to sit. As she sits she picks at everything she can see. The hair on her legs is growing back, tiny black dots at her ankles like they've been stippled with pen.

She has a new spot coming in at her temple; it's still beneath the skin so she can't pop it, but she can feel the swell and pull of it. Her fringe won't lie flat and there's a stupid kink at her crown. She rubs her legs together and the stubble rasps. Well, while she's here.

She gets the razor and soap and rests her left foot up on the sink. Maybe she could waft the shit smell out with a towel? She doesn't even know if it smells any more or she's only imagining it.

When she first tried shaving her legs, aged ten, her mum noticed the missing razor and asked her what she was shaving. Stokeley had been confused by that, unsure what other body parts on a woman would need shaving.

She'd expected a lecture about how she was too young to be doing things like that, but her mum hadn't been annoyed or finger-wagging; she had left a long thoughtful pause and then said to always use shaving gel or hair conditioner so she wouldn't get a rash.

Her mum had died the next year, before Stokeley had a need to shave any other parts of herself. She was in a coma for two months before they switched the machines off, long enough for her leg hair to grow in so long it wasn't stubbly any more, but soft and strokeable, which Stokeley discovered in after-school visiting hours, perched on the edge of the bed in intensive care, trying to find a part of her mum that wasn't attached to wires, settling for the few inches of leg visible between her socks and her pyjama bottoms.

Stokeley runs the tap for ages but it doesn't get warm, so she shaves with cold water. She wishes she could take a pill that would make all her body hair fall out except for on her head and her eyebrows. Though there's always wigs and eyebrow pencils.

She catches her ankle bone with the razor and blood beads. She swipes it with her fingertip and lifts it to her mouth, sucking the blood off.

Her pubes, though – is it better to have no pubes at all? The models at the museum had pubes, but they were from olden times and things were different then. She knows waxing and shaving is the correct thing to do to pubes but she doesn't know how much.

She wants to ask Delilah.

She won't ask Delilah.

*

The dwarfs had a glass coffin made, so she could be seen from all sides. They laid her inside, and with golden letters wrote on it her name, and that she was a princess.

*

When Stokeley gets home from the trip to the anatomy museum, her dad is just back from work. Friday night means sports and chicken while sitting in his chair. Stokeley hates his chair. It has grease marks on the armrests because he doesn't use a napkin when he eats. Every week Stokeley washes the cloth that hangs over the chair back and absorbs the grease from his hair. She always picks it up by the corners so she doesn't have the touch the part that he touched.

'Did you bring it?'

Stokeley doesn't reply, just holds out the clear bag, still warm in her hand. The roast chicken inside is pressing its stubby wings against the sides of the bag as if trying to get out. Caught up in the smell of it is the beginning of the smell of the shit her dad will do after he's eaten it.

'You're such a good girl. Will you have some too?'

Stokeley shakes her head; she never has some, and they both know it.

'I love to treat you to this. You know I love you.'

Stokeley doesn't really think it's a treat for her if she doesn't have any, but she doesn't reply. She brings her dad a plate and cutlery, but there's no point. He rips the body apart with his hands, lifting each part delicately to his grease-smeared mouth, selecting strips with his front teeth.

Stokeley thinks about her mum, and how she'd looked beautiful lying there in her hospital bed, even with all the wires and beeps and the thing on her face to make her breathe. Her mum was always moving, always talking on the phone or saying to Stokeley *put your shoes on* or *have you brushed your teeth?* or *once upon a time* or *not now, darling.* Maybe she'd always been beautiful but Stokeley hadn't had a chance to look. Never in her life had Stokeley been able to just sit and look at her mum's face. Before, if she'd had to draw it from memory, or provide a police photofit image, she couldn't have done it. But in stillness, she saw clearly every bit of her mum's beauty.

Later, after the chicken has caused her dad to do some loud and stinking shit, he will sit in his chair and call her over, and say:

'You're a good girl, Stokeley, you're a good daughter, I love you, do you know I love you? It's just me and you, you're the only thing that keeps me going. I love you, do you love me too, do you know how much I love you? You're a good girl and you deserve a good man. Daughters marry men like their fathers and you'll make a man like me happy one day, so very happy.'

The chicken is down to the bones. Her dad sucks each bone into his mouth, lustfully, goatishly, a slight moan in his throat. As Stokeley watches him, her gore rises; she vomits into her mouth and swallows it, keeping her face expressionless.

*

You're a good girl.

*

Between their perfect, up-tipped breasts is a Y-incision, the skin is spread open like an exotic flower, pink and yellow petals specked with red. Peeping out from inside, the gleam of the intact breast-bone, a row of pearls stitched onto red velvet.

There is no odour, no fluid. Nothing leaks or sags or gets misshapen. They were perfect when they were cast in wax, and they are still perfect now.

The organs inside can be removed and then handled, examined, replaced. In one uterus, a tiny wax foetus. In some the skin is shown peeled back, revealing the striations of muscle and fat inside, the twine of blood vessels. In some an arm or leg is severed partway, showing the penny-sized circle of bone centred in the meat. There are redheads and blondes and brunettes.

Every head is tipped back. Every limb is flatteringly bent. Every mouth is red.

They are as beautiful as women in paintings. More beautiful, even, because they look so solid, so real, like proper dead girls.

*

And she lay there in the coffin a long, long time, and she did not decay, but looked like she was asleep, for she was still as white as snow and as red as blood, and as black-haired as ebony.

*

'You be the vampire, Stokes,' says Marybeth. She got them all hooked on paranormal romances; Stokeley didn't actually like them that much initially, until she found that in some of them the girl got to be the vampire or werewolf or fae creature or whatever.

Of course that then raised the question of why a werewolf-girl would be interested in a boring, hairless, lukewarm human boy, but still.

'I was the vampire last time,' complains Stokeley, though weakly, because actually she prefers to be the vampire and doesn't understand why the others don't want to be.

'Well, that means you've had practice so you'll be good at it,' snaps back Casey.

'Fine. But you can do the blood.' Stokeley, reaching for the red lipstick, addresses this to Delilah, then loses her nerve and hands the black plastic tube to Casey.

Casey paints Stokeley's lips while the others swoon across Stokeley's bed, complete with sighing sound effects. They don't have flowing muslin gowns but they make do with bed sheets.

Stokeley holds her blanket at the top corners, swooping round the room.

'I'm a bat, a big bad bat, and I am batty for you!'

Casey sniggers.

'Come on, Stokeley!' Marybeth is unamused; she has found the perfect swooning pose and won't even open her eyes. 'Do it properly.'

Unseen by the others in the darkened room, Stokeley lowers her wings. She tilts her head down. She pushes out her throat to lower her voice.

'Your blood,' she murmurs, 'smells delicious. Your lips tempt me. I must have a bite.'

She lifts her wings and strides towards the bed, thinking: be sexy, be strong, be the vampirest vampire.

'Your skin is warm and I am so cold. The centuries alone have chilled me to my bones. Warm me, sweet girl, with your hot blood.'

Is that too far? She glances along the row of ready faces but no one is smiling. Not too far, then.

'I am coming for your blood. I will taste you now.'

The vampire's kiss comes to them all, in the shape of two lipsticked dots at their throats. As each girl feels the dap of the lipstick, they let out an exaggerated, fake-sexy moan.

'Oh, vampire! How cold you are!'

'I'll never be the same after this kiss!'

'Is my blood the sweetest? Will you love me forever?'

Afterwards they all sit up, giggling and fake-swooning, not quite managing to look Stokeley in the eye. She's still holding on to her blanket-wings; she wants to wrap her arms around herself, enclose herself. Instead she leaps off the bed, wings aloft, and runs around the room cawing like a seagull.

'I'm the bat!' she sings. 'The battiest bat! A rounders bat covered in bats!'

Marybeth pouts and Delilah rolls her eyes, but Casey and Zeke join in, running around the room flapping their sheets like wings, pretending to be part of the first all-bat Olympic rounders team. They all take care not to rub off the marks of love the vampire left on their necks.

They eventually fall asleep like that, wrapped in their sheets, red dots smearing into their pillows, laid out on a heap of duvets across Stokeley's bedroom floor.

*

You're so pretty like that.

*

Sometime in the night, Delilah got up, maybe to go to the toilet or maybe to look at the stars or maybe to have another go at the vampire game, or maybe for another reason entirely, but we can never really know what goes on in a young girl's mind, but whatever her reason she climbed over her sleeping friends until she got to Stokeley, who really did look pretty like that, her lipstick faded so it looked like her mouth was naturally reddened, the concealer and blush blended by her pillow so it looked like her real skin but better, and for Delilah's own reasons she looked at the sleeping girl and she bent down so she could breathe in her breath, which smelled sweet and specific, and she leaned closer and closer and closer and Stokeley's lips were open a little in sleep, just slightly, and her tongue was caught between her teeth, the pink peep of it, and Delilah smiled and poked her own tongue out a little in response, and because she was so close her tongue touched Stokeley's lip, and she turned her head to the side like men in films did so their noses wouldn't bump and she closed that final millimetre, thinking of the bit in the story she had only just remembered from a book she'd read as a little kid, where a kiss from a prince has the power to wake a princess, and who wants to be a princess anyway these days when you could be a queen, regal, elegant, unmoving, and Stokeley's lips were soft and her breath stopped and *Delilah what the fuck*, Marybeth's voice half laughing and half angry, not sure whether an accusation was needed, already thinking in the manic glee of playground taunts, but Delilah's face looked scared, *I don't think she's breathing,* and Marybeth crawled across the duvets and knelt on Stokeley's bed to peer at her, *what do you mean, what's wrong with her, wake up, Stokes, wake the fuck up,* and it did smell a little like shit in the room but only barely, only a slight remnant that seemed to be in all the soft furnishings, mostly it smelled of body spray and sleep breath, sweet and a little stale, *don't shake her like that Casey jesus christ you'll give her brain damage* and even though it did seem like Stokeley wasn't breathing they still all thought she was winding them up, it was clear in the way they were overdramatising, because it's exciting, isn't it, the spectacle of things, like TV but right in front of you and people you know, even when it's sad or difficult there's still a strange appeal to it, *she's already got brain damage you idiot why won't she wake up*, and we can all think several things at once, and while they were all thinking some small worries about their friend, they were also thinking that she always had to be a drama queen and make it all about her, and that at school on Monday they'd make it a certain kind of story, a little mean to Stokeley but not too mean, just kind of knowing and eye-rolling, what is she like, the way you can be when you know someone really well, *Stokes please it's not funny wake uuuuuup*, and Stokeley's dad heard the commotion and came running in, a tartan dressing gown with the hem ripped and the belt untied, his unmatching pyjamas, and they had to explain to him what was happening, how she wouldn't wake, and although their voices were overlapping and high and their hands flapped they weren't scared now, because her dad would fix things, but their calm instantly flipped over to terror because Stokeley's dad wasn't reacting right, not in a way that adults should, adults who are always calm and fix things, whatever is wrong they fix it, but Stokeley's dad is at the side of Stokeley's bed, rocking back on his heels, clutching at Stokeley's hair and pawing at her face, moaning and wailing *not her, not her too, I can't lose her too,* and the girls all back away in horror, hands to their mouths, backing up until their bare heels hit the wall, eyes wide and staring at Stokeley's dad in his grief, how it's too close and too real and they don't like it, they don't want it, they wish he is behind glass, safe and distant and observable, and all the lights go on and all the duvets are pushed to the side to clear the floor and someone goes to call an ambulance and someone else goes next door for the neighbour and

205

someone else remembers the first-aid training from school, and it's bright and noise and heat, and at the circle of this torrent of movement and fuss is Stokeley, motionless, hair dark against the pale pink of her much-laundered pillow.

Her back is caught in a slight arch. Her skin is ivory, poreless.

Her eyes are tilted half open. Her mouth is caught in a smile.

And she is so, so beautiful.

I've started leaving the light on in my cabin at night. At first I left the light on in the studio too, but then I could see it from my bedroom window, and I didn't like that. I felt that if I didn't keep looking at it, it would move away from me, that tiny yellow glow swallowed up by the night. Then I worried that if I did keep looking at it, it would move away anyway.

I go for walks at night and it's black, black, black. All cloud, no stars. I might as well be an abandoned ship, tilted and floating on the night ocean. If I stand still and hold my breath, I get seasick.

Sometimes I forget to breathe. I think I forget to eat too. I tried to go to the shop today, but it was shut. Or maybe that was yesterday. I tapped on the sliding glass doors, but all the lights were off inside. There's nothing on the shelves even, just some cardboard boxes slumping musty in the corners. But there were things there before, I'm sure there were, and people and tills and lights and an Icelandic easy-listening radio station on the tannoy.

My hands are shaking. When I blink, the world jolts to the side. There is the door to my cabin. It's open.

Sweeter Than the Tongue
I Remember

The heat and the dreams came together. All afternoon a warm rain fell, churning the grassy parks into mud and making my toes slide out of my sandal straps. All night sweat itched along my ribs like walking flies, slicking across my shoulder blades, along my top lip, off the tips of my hair. All morning the washing machine grumbled with the night's soaked sheets. I slept like I was at the bottom of the sea; I needed three alarm clocks to wake. But with sleep came dreams.

Pleasant at first: a man with black eyes and soft hands. Skin-touching, mouth-kissing. Like a sleazy film with all the narrative cut and only the dirty bits left. I'd been single for a while, and the dreams were a thrill. The man in my dreams looked like every man I had ever desired: the star of my favourite film, my high-school boyfriend, my father. Every night he pushed me further until the clamour of my alarm pulled me, sweating and exhausted, away from him.

In those early days I felt naive, coveted. My lips were always swollen, my throat raw. Colleagues teased me about my secret lover and I didn't correct them. I liked my new glow.

One night, mid-orgasm, with my legs bent impossibly and my blood soaring high, I changed my mind. *No*, I said. *No*. Suddenly I didn't want the man and I didn't want to come and I didn't want to twist my body that way and I didn't want, didn't want.

But the man did want. So that was that.

My dreams were vivid, and I woke with reddened thighs and catfight scratches along my collarbones. There was only one solution that I could see. He came for me in my sleep; I would not sleep.

I tried coffee and sugar and vigorous exercise. Bright lights, spicy food, long night walks, splashing my face with cold water, a variety of substances sold by a friend of a friend.

It only took a few days for my constant wakefulness to affect me. My fingers started twitching, spilling drops from my coffee cup onto the carpet. Words jumped across the page as I tried to read them. I couldn't tell if traffic lights were red or green; I just crossed my fingers and accelerated through them.

Sometimes, in the afternoon heat haze, I'd blink and my eyes wouldn't open again. The man lurked at the edges of my vision, his heavy hands over my eyes. I'd wake with a shout or fall off my chair.

Finally a friend, noticing my shadowed eyes and clumsy steps, sent me to her doctor. I'd thought he was just a GP, but he made me stare at a metronome and asked about my childhood. I don't know what I wanted from him: special pills, a golden key, magic beans? Something, anything.

When he asked about my nightmares, I told him all the stories I could think up. I told him about eight-legged beasties, sitting exams naked, falling from mile-high rooftops. But it didn't take long for my tired mind to run out of nightmares. I couldn't even remember what normal people dreamed about any more, and my exhausted brain refused to invent new terrors to tell him about. Meaning to tell a lie, out of my mouth came the truth.

The doctor smiled, restful and soft.

'I can make it better,' he said. We made a date for Friday.

That was three nights away. I spent them standing by my kitchen window, sucking on ice cubes. When I started to nod off, I bit down.

At the restaurant, the doctor ordered for me. He fed the food to me in bites. Afterwards, he took me back to his place. The sex was like watching a porn film: unreal and too real, out of focus and full of close-ups. His last kiss contained three tiny, sugared pills, from his tongue to mine.

I slept. It was empty and silent and perfect.

I was pulled away from nothing by the doctor's alarm clock. Dozing beside me, he looked like he belonged in a piazza: marble-cold, marble-still. I pressed my back against his. I wanted to absorb his cold, but I would settle for him taking my heat. The doctor went to work, and I called in sick and stayed in his bed, eating waffles and reading his out-of-date magazines as the rain pattered at the windows. He came home with a brand-new raincoat in my size.

For a week, I stayed dry and clean. Around me, the raining city festered, fruit peel and flowers starting to rot. But I slept blankly every night against the doctor's marble-cold back. His skin smelled of nothing. His last kiss was always sweet with pills. I had to bring my own alarm clock from home, as his alone wasn't enough to wake me.

The doorbell pulled me from a dreamless sleep. The bed was empty; the doctor had gone to work already. I opened the door and held out my hand for the post, but the skinny man on the doorstep was not holding any envelopes. He had shadows under his eyes and was biting flakes of dry skin off his lips. Suddenly I wished I'd left the chain on the door.

'Yes?'

'Take me back.'

'I'm sorry?' I moved so that the door was between us.

'Please. I deserve another chance.'

'Just give me the post.'

'I love you. Don't do this.'

'I think you have the wrong ... ' I stared at his face. 'Have we met?'

He laughed, but it turned into a cough. 'You know we have.'

I slammed the door and ran into the kitchen.

How could it be him? How could this be real? Maybe I never woke up at all.

I turned on the shower as hot as it would go, and stood in the water with my eyes shut. I couldn't look down; if I saw my own skin, I'd see his hands on it.

When I walked out of the bathroom I stopped breathing. Through the stained glass in the front door I saw him: leaning on the door frame, smoking, his back to me. How long had he been there? Should I call the police? A friend? The doctor?

I put the chain on the door and inched it open.

'What do you want?'

He spun round and flicked his cigarette into the flower bed. 'You.' He exhaled his lungful of smoke. 'I just want you. I miss you.' He reached out a hand and I pushed the door so that I could only see him out of one eye.

'I don't know who you are and I don't know what you want. You must have me confused with someone else.'

He smiled, his eyes shining. His T-shirt pulled tight across his chest, bulked out by his muscled arms. I saw then that there was no need to be afraid of this man. No need to close a door against him. He didn't want anything from me except to kiss me with that pouting red mouth, put those strong hands around my waist, touch my...

Red mouth? When I first opened the door, he was biting flakes of skin off his lips. They were pale, thin and unhealthy-looking, like the rest of him. I scrunched my eyes shut so tight that green and orange lines wavered behind my lids. I opened them, properly awake, and stared at his chapped lips and scrawny arms. His smile was gone.

'I'm asking you nicely,' he said.

'Leave me alone.' I slammed the door and stood in the middle of the hall, watching his shadow as he stood on the doorstep.

'You love me!' he shouted through the letter box. 'You know you do!'

I watched his blurry shape through the stained glass until he skulked off.

The doctor suggested repressed memories, an overactive imagination. He suggested I'd dreamed the whole thing: a by-product of my insomnia.

'I've been sleeping fine for weeks! Ever since you... since we...'

Even to my ears, it sounded petulant. I stopped talking and he carried me to the bedroom. *No*, I said. *No*. Sleep came for me.

I woke at dawn, shivering with sweat. I felt wet and aching, fever cramps between my legs. My dreams slunk away beneath the sheets.

The doctor was already up, clattering cups in the kitchen. I heard the low mumble of talk radio, the white noise of morning traffic.

I got ready to leave, then checked my bag – wallet, keys, phone – and opened the front door. On the doorstep stood the skinny man in a dirty blue tracksuit. He was biting his lips and tapping a cigarette against the door, watching the sparks fly.

'Aren't you going to invite me in?'

He licked his lips and stepped closer. He looked like a film star, my high-school boyfriend, my father.

I closed my eyes and pressed my knuckles against them, counting my breaths as the colours flashed across my vision. When I looked again, I saw a stained tracksuit, sallow skin, bloodshot eyes.

I locked the front door behind me and stalked to my car without looking back. In the rear-view mirror I saw him sit down on the doctor's doorstep and pull out a cigarette.

Every night I take my sugar-kiss pills and sleep beside my cold marble doctor, who I do not desire. Every morning I walk past the ghost of a dream, who I do and then don't and then do desire. I can't have both of them. I don't think I want either. But *no* is such a small word.

I don't remember the houses here having lights on. I don't remember the shop having food in it. I don't remember anyone else being in the pool. I don't remember a car passing on the road.

I go for walks; I walk down the road until my legs start to shake, then I walk back. I never reach anywhere.

I leave the lights on in my cabin but when I get back they're always off. I don't bother to lock the door any more, as no one else is here - and if someone had come in, surely they couldn't still be hiding. Could they?

It's hot tonight. I'll open the window.

Watch the Wall, My Darling, While the Gentlemen Go By

He takes you from the alley behind a club where you've gone to throw up because you don't want your friends to see. You're drunk and were probably flirting with a stranger and your skirt is rucked up in a way both slutty and unflattering, making you simultaneously desirable and disgusting to any man who might happen by and see you. And how is a man supposed to react to that? Take a moment to think of all the things you did to bring yourself here.

He comes at you gun-fast with his arms full of plastic sheeting and snowballs you into his back seat. With the plastic wrapped around your head, your flailing sounds very loud. The car is bumping and spinning but it might be your head. You're so sure that you're suffocating that you don't even scream. You don't struggle against him, only against the plastic sheeting, which is a mistake as the plastic sheeting isn't really the problem.

You've heard stories of girls tricked into cars by a man wearing a fake leg cast, asking for help with heavy bags; girls tricked into cars to help with injured dogs; girls tricked into cars because they looked like taxis but were just some man's car. He didn't even bother using a trick on you, and really, what does that say about you? You're worse than all of those girls. You weren't even worth making up a lie.

You hadn't had a chance to throw up in the alley before he got you and you do it now, into the plastic sheeting, and there's nowhere for it to go so it all goes back on you. This makes you more disgusting than desirable, and you can't help thinking that maybe that's safer.

He drives for a long time and you pass out for a bit and dream that you're not in his car, that you're still out with your friends, that you're at home asleep with a hangover already starting, but when he stops you jolt awake and you really are in his car.

Why didn't you signal for help? Why didn't you break all your nails trying to open the door? Why didn't you smash the car window and throw yourself out into the traffic, dead maybe but at least not raped? How useless you are. You have learned nothing. But don't worry, you'll have plenty of time to learn now.

He puts a cloth that stinks of chemicals over your mouth and nose, and the last thing you hear is him calling you Dove, which isn't your name but perhaps it could be.

You wake in a pit. You think it might be a dried-up well. Above you, blue sky, a few clouds. He must have dragged you over rocky ground to get you here because your shoulders ache in their sockets and your heels are torn and bloody, your shoes long gone. The sides of the pit are as high as your apartment building and made of smooth stone. You rub at the stone but there are no finger holds, and it's too wide for you to brace your body and climb up. You surprise yourself at how readily you abandon the idea of climbing out.

Remember when you read that thing on the internet and then decided you weren't going to move out of the way of men in the street any more? You were always going to walk in a straight line, and you'd only move out of the way for buggies and old ladies and dogs. Even when you walked towards a man with calm purpose and he walked towards you without even noticing you, and you both ended up coming to a halt in the middle of the street, you with a polite smile and him surprised, confused – still you didn't move, still you didn't excuse yourself. Eventually the man would move aside and you'd walk on, feeling strong, feeling tall, feeling like you should write a blog post about this. And where did it get you? All that reading, all that purposeful walking? A pit in the woods.

He says he's going to get you clean. He says that you'll see how good you can be when you're his clean girl, all nice on the inside. No drugs, no filth. You're not on drugs but it doesn't really matter. Who you used to be then is not who you used to be now. And who you will be after this is different again.

He turns the hose on you. You shriek and fight, so he keeps it on you for so long that the dirt at the bottom of the pit gets muddy and churned, swallowing your ankles. Because of that, later the cuts on your feet get infected and he has to inject you with antibiotics, which isn't fun as you have to tie a bag on your head and truss your own wrists before he'll rope-lift you out of the pit. Why can't anything be easy with you? You learn from that, and from then on you strip down ready for the hose and stand X-shaped so you can be cleaned quickly. It's just easier.

The first time he lifts you out of the pit and into the house to do things to you, you feel incredulous, unreal, trying not to laugh as the hysteria bubbles up your throat because this can't possibly be happening to you. Any minute now the story will be over, the credits will roll, he'll say it was all a joke, run along home now. But the story isn't over, because it isn't a story, and he does the very worst things to you, worse even than you could have imagined, and there's nothing you can do about it. Afterwards he puts you back in the pit and your blood drips into the dirt.

The second time he does things to you, you feel very very sad.

The third time, angry.

The fourth, resigned.

The fifth, you feel nothing at all.

After that you lose count. Once or twice you almost enjoy it, or at least you don't mind it so much. It's nice to be out of the pit.

You do try various escape methods. Going at his throat with a butter knife, trying to trip him with the rope, smiling and simpering and then suddenly launching yourself at him all teeth and nails. But he's big and he's strong and he's a man, and what the fuck are you?

He tells you over and over that you need to be better, you need to be selfless and forgiving and nurturing and beautiful and graceful and you need to smile, just fucking smile for once, why can't you ever be happy? And so you try, and you get better at it, though never quite good enough. If you'd known to be all these things in the first place then he wouldn't have to teach you. You have no one to blame but yourself.

And if it's painful and humiliating, well, women are good at that, aren't we? Menstrual cramps, internal exams, childbirth: we mustn't complain now, must we? It's all normal. You should be glad it's not worse, he tells you. He's done worse to others, and he could do it again; but maybe he won't. He likes you. He wants you to last longer than any of them. And isn't that, actually, unexpectedly, kind of sweet? He likes you the best. You are the best woman out of all the women. Congratulations.

You're in the pit for a long time. Summer ends and dead leaves fall into the pit. Autumn ends and the pit fills up with rain. Your old blankets rot and he gives you new ones. At some point he lowers a wooden table into the pit so that you can lie on top of it to sleep, and under it when it rains. You don't think you've ever been more grateful for anything in your life.

Now your hair is bracken and your bones jut and your breath reeks of death, and you didn't need to read all those blog posts because if you were to walk down the street you could be as straight or as crooked as you liked and every single man would cross the street to get away from you. Why did you fight so hard when all that effort only brought you here? Though if you think about it, perhaps here was the place you were meant to be all along. And if you think about it some more, doesn't it feel nice to give up the fight? Isn't it a relief, really, despite the slight discomfort, to just exist?

And then, one day, he lets you go. He says that you're his Dove and you must fly.

At first you just stand in his kitchen, barefoot, blinking. He pushes you. Then he pushes you harder.

You stumble out of his house and through the yard and past the cars and through the trees. You didn't think you had the strength left to run but you do, and you feel a sound building inside you, from your feet right up to your throat, and you let it go and it spurs you on, and you're screaming and laughing and it's over, it's over, you're alive and it's over.

You reach the road and you try to flag down a car, any car. It must be around midday because the sun is right above you and the air is warm enough that you sweat, your waving arms airing out your stale body.

The road isn't busy but a few cars do pass, swerving to get around you. The drivers stare at you in the rear-view. They're confused and scared and you wait for them to drive back for you but they don't.

And let's think about this: you're standing in the middle of the road shrieking and naked and, let's be honest, with all those sores and sticky-out bones you look like you're in the end stages of the plague. Would you stop for you?

And finally, finally, a car stops, and relief gushes through you like ice water and your knees soften and you drop, the ground welcomes you and you're laughing and crying and you tilt your face up to say thank you, thank you.

And the car door opens and the driver gets out and walks towards you, and of course it's him, you knew it would be him, it couldn't be anyone else other than him.

So you get up off your knees. You climb into the car. You let him take you back.

Acknowledgements

Thank you for the writing time, space and beautiful surroundings: Creative Scotland / Gullkistan Residency for Creative People, Iceland / Cove Park, Scotland / Granada UNESCO City of Literature Writer in Residence, Spain

Thank you for the feedback and writing dates:
Sasha DeBuyl / Camilla Grudova / Nadine Aisha Jassat / Alex Kahler / Katy McAulay / Susie McConnell / Paul McQuade / Andrea Mullaney / Heather Parry / Rachael Stephen / Angela Sutton / Ryan Vance

Thank you for the story inspiration:
Camilla Grudova for the pica / Robin Haig for the bat-bath / Paul McQuade for the fox piss / Gab Paananen for the mushrooms

Thank you for making this book a reality:
Elizabeth Foley at Harvill Secker / Cathryn Summerhayes at Curtis Brown

And thank you to Annie, always.

First publications:

'Second Fear' in 'My Body Cannot Forget Your Body': *Banshee Lit*

'Sleep, You Black-eyed Pig, Fall into a Deep Pit of Ghosts: *F(r)iction*

'Third Fear' in 'Last One to Leave Please Turn Off the Lights': *Copper Nickel*

'Fourth Fear' in 'Last One to Leave Please Turn Off the Lights': commissioned by New Writing North for the BBC Free Thinking Festival in 2017

'Things My Wife and I Found Hidden in Our House': *This Dreaming Isle*

'We Can Make Something Grow Between the Mushrooms and the Snow': *The Puritan*

'My House is Out Where the Lights End': *Nightscript*

'Good Good Good, Nice Nice Nice': *The Shadow Booth*

'The Only Time I Think of You is All the Time': Monstrous Regiment

penguin.co.uk/vintage